RIVERS
OF TIME

The Black Coat Script Library

RIVERS OF TIME

A Screenplay by
Roy Thomas

From a Story by
Roy Thomas & Janis Hendler

Based on the Book by
L. Sprague de Camp

A Black Coat Press Book

Acknowledgements: We are indebted to Arthur Lieberman, *Conan*'s own attorney, for his help in arranging for the publication of this screenplay, Brian K. Morris for retyping the typescript and David McDonnell for proofreading it.

This screenplay is based on the stories by L. Sprague de Camp which appeared in the 1993 volume *Rivers of Time*, published by Baen Books, and is published by permission of the De Camp Family Limited Partnership.

Visit our website at www.blackcoatpress.com

Introduction

In the early 1990s, with Steven Spielberg's *Jurassic Park* setting box-office records, I decided that perhaps the time was ripe to try to sell a screenplay based on a favorite short story of mine, L. Sprague de Camp's "A Gun for Dinosaur." I had always liked that tale of Reginald Rivers, big game hunter who helped well-heeled clients stalk the big reptilians via time machine, and who explained to a prospective client that he wouldn't take him hunting because he was "just not big enough to handle a gun for dinosaur."

De Camp himself had explained years before that his tale was written as a reaction to what he considered "scientific errors" in the famous Ray Bradbury short story "A Sound of Thunder"–although, being the gentleman he was, Sprague would never mention Bradbury or his story by name. It was one of those happy cases where someone producing an "answer" to a popular work of art created a *new* work of art–not unlike the way Howard Hawks directed the movie *Rio Bravo* as a response to Fred Zinnemann's *High Noon,* and American Cinema was twice as well off for having both of them. So with Bradbury and de Camp.

Written in 1956, "A Gun for Dinosaur" had long since proved one of the most enduringly popular stories ever penned by de Camp, who became a selling and respected author of both fantasy and science fiction in the late 1930s and 1940s. It had been dramatized on the *X Minus One* radio show when the story was quite new (and dramatic radio, alas, was old and feeble). In fact, I myself had, with Sprague's permission, adapted the tale into a 14-page comic book story in *Worlds Unknown* No. 2 (July 1973) when I was Marvel Comics' editor-in-chief. I had met him and his wife Catherine twice in connection with *Conan the Barbarian*, whose adventures de Camp had continued and marketed in the 1960s. They, my wife Dann and I, had all been on hand to applaud the night

"*The Conan and Red Sonja Show*" opened at Universal Studios.

Contacting Sprague, I was overjoyed to learn that "A Gun for Dinosaur" was now part of a recently-released paperback volume from Baen Books with the evocative title *Rivers of Time*. Apparently, his colleague Robert Silverberg had invited him in 1990 to write a dinosaur story for his own proposed anthology, *The Ultimate Dinosaur*. "Feeling that Reginald Rivers ought to have many good tales to tell besides 'A Gun for Dinosaur,' " de Camp related later, "I wrote 'Crocamander Ques*t*' for Bob." Soon afterward, obviously enjoying himself, he wrote five more Rivers stories, all published between 1991-93 in the digests *Analog* and *Asimov's Science Fiction Magazine*. Later, to fill out the Baen book, he added two more.

With the aid of my then-agent Daniel Ostroff (now a film producer himself of such well-received fare as *Snow in August,* made from Pete Hamill's novel), a deal was struck whereby my then-writing partner Janis Hendler and I could represent *Rivers of Time* as a screen property. Janis, who had written and produced for such TV series as *Knight Rider* and *The Fall Guy,* among others, became as big a fan of the material as I was, and we made it our special mission to try to get a film made of the Rivers saga while Sprague was still around to enjoy it.

Alas, we didn't quite make it. A number of Hollywood producers expressed interest of one kind or another, but in spite of successful post-*Jurassic Park* potboilers such as *Carnosaur,* they seemed reluctant to walk where Spielberg had trod. Perhaps the potential big budget for such a picture had something to do with it. Naturally, some of these producers had their own "creative" suggestions to make the film more palatable. "Can you do it without dinosaurs?" one asked in all seriousness. I was reminded of the USAF officer in Joseph Heller's novel *Catch-22* who asked the chaplain if he could write a prayer without any reference in it to God. Joe Heller must have often been reminded of situations in his masterpiece when he was writing in Tinseltown in the 1960s. I know I was, in the '80s.

One producer was especially responsive to the material, however. I seem to recall that he was a recently-deposed studio head with an independent production deal–just like every recently-deposed studio head since the days when Sam Goldwyn became just the G in MGM. This producer made a handshake deal with Janis and me for *Rivers of Time*–but, to paraphrase the aforementioned Goldwyn, a handshake deal isn't worth the paper it's written on. While our agent was negotiating with the producer over a difference between our positions of $3000 in a six-figure deal, he–our agent–suddenly got a phone call from said producer's business agent (naturally, not from the producer himself) to say that the producer had spent all his money on another project and the deal was off. We might have sued, but what would that have gotten us? So it was back to square one.

By now, Janis and I had a general storyline we were happy with. It altered de Camp's character and situation considerably, but we felt it was true to the spirit of the material. Gone, of necessity, was the notion that Rivers was a middle-aged Australian. Too old... and too limited in the casting. Did we really want to write a movie whose only viable choice for star was Paul Hogan? Besides, did we truly want to be churlish about it if Tom Cruise decided he could see himself hunting dinosaurs in the Cretaceous?

Along with the new material we added, Janis and I took ideas primarily from two of de Camp's nine Rivers stories: "A Gun for Dinosaur" itself, with August Holtzinger and a bigwig criminal named Courtney James (whose name we changed to Desmond Swayzey) and his girl friend, whose part we expanded greatly–and "The Big Splash," about an expedition back in time to witness the K-T Event, which some (but not all) scientists believe caused the extinction of the dinosaurs. You'll find Ming the Cook and Beauregard (forerunner of Bo Black) in the original de Camp stories, too. And, for reasons I forget just now, we changed Rivers' partner from Chandra

Aiyar (a.k.a. "the Raja"), an Indian from India, to an American "Indian" named Alex Blackelk. There are nods in there, as well, to the likes of *Brick Bradford* (the time-traveling comic strip hero) and V.T. Hamlin, the creator of *Alley Oop,* and a few other things I'll let you find for yourself.

The other major conscious choice Janis and I made was to concoct our story in the vein of the classic tough-guy-and-tougher-gal mode of some of the great movies of the 1930s, such as *Red Dust* and *China Seas* and *Too Hot to Handle.* The male star of all three of these was Clark Gable, always opposite Jean Harlow or some other tough cookie who could hold her own with him. We'd like to think Harlow wouldn't have minded playing Willow Lamar... and Gable in his heyday would've made a good Rivers, come to that.

Eventually, as prospective producers dried up, I decided sometime in the latter half of the 1990s simply to sit down and write a screenplay based on Janis' and my adaptive story–because how else could I totally see it in my head–even *read* the damn thing? Janis understandably opted to let me write away at that point, but to me *Rivers of Time* is still very much the work of both of us.

And of L. Sprague de Camp, who I suspect molded the original, urbane Reginald Rivers rather after himself.

What can I say? I may be prejudiced, but I'd still rather watch *Rivers of Time* at my local Cineplex than most of what's playing there this week.

Even if I *am* too small to handle a gun for dinosaur.

Roy Thomas

L. SPRAGUE DE CAMP

The Adventures of Reginald Rivers
Time Traveller Extraordinaire!

RIVERS OF TIME

72195-X · CAN $6.50 · U.S $4.99

Rivers of Time

FADE IN:

<u>EXT. THE LATE TRIASSIC - DAY</u>
Sunlight falls upon a scattering of cycads and seed-ferns around a large standing pool of water–an oasis amid an arid landscape glimpsed just beyond the vegetation. In this stillness no birds sing–because no birds yet exist.

SUPERIMPOSED/BOTTOM: THE TRIASSIC - 225 MILLION YEARS AGO.

A rat-like mammal (a MEGAZOSTRODON, six inches long) creeps warily to the pool's edge–hesitates, then begins to drink.

Suddenly, a long thin snout flashes from the dark water– crocodilian jaws CLAMP shut on the mammal–a five-foot-long RUTIODON (resembling a caiman) flounders onto shore. A beat.

Then, without warning, the fanged jaws of an ERYTHRO-SUCHUS swoop down from above and engulf the young Rutiodon.

The bulky 15-footer up-ends the croc and swallows it, till only its tail sticks out–then that, too, is engorged.

At the SOUND of a cracking twig, the Erythro turns. With a ROAR half bellow, half bird-screech, it charges on four legs through the shallow water, toward the far end of the oasis.

BLAM! A large red hole appears over the Erythro's heart. The reptile is momentarily slowed, but keeps moving.

BLAM! A second wound near the first. The beast takes a last faltering step–falls dead, half-in, half-out of the pool.

> FLETCHER (O.S.)
> I got him! I got him!

Three armed men in safari garb approach the carcass. TIMO-THY FLETCHER (50s), overweight, puffing, hefts a smoking, double-barreled Continental .600 rifle, like those the others carry.

ALEX BLACKELK (40ish), a burly Sioux, keeps an eye out for predators. He moves gracefully despite his size.

Clearly in charge is REG RIVERS (mid-30s), ruggedly hand-some, cut from the same cloth as the great hunters of legend–an Allan Quatermain for the early 21st century.

> FLETCHER
> See, Rivers? I told you I'd get one first try!

> RIVERS
> And I told you to hold your fire. That's an Erythro-suchus.

> FLETCHER
> An Ery-what?

> ALEX
> You paid to shoot a Teratosaur–just the size head to mount over your fireplace, you said.

> FLETCHER
> You mean that's not–?

Alex kicks the carcass' head as if it were a car's tire.

ALEX

A Terato's a lot faster and meaner, and walks on two
legs.

RIVERS
(looking O.S.)
Like that.

A ROAR O.S. louder than the Erythro. Alex and Fletcher
whirl.

A 25 feet-long TERATOSAURUS lopes across the arid landscape outside the oasis—it spots the humans.

Rivers grins wryly at the gaping Fletcher.

RIVERS
(continuing)
He's all yours, Mr. Fletcher.

Fletcher raises his rifle, aims, fires. CLICK! Nothing.

FLETCHER
It's jammed! You shoot it!

The ROARING Terato charges—

Alex, rifle ready, glances anxiously from Rivers to the Terato.
Rivers raises his .600 slowly, getting it in his sights as if he
had all day. To Fletcher:

RIVERS
Your call. But if I do, that counts as your trophy
head.

Fletcher impulsively deflects Rivers' rifle barrel downward.

                    FLETCHER
        Like hell it does!

                    RIVERS
        Then this safari is officially over.

Alex heads through the vegetation bordering the pool. Rivers
shoves Fletcher, to start his petrified client moving.

The Teratosaur charges in after them, ROARING.

BORDERING THE POOL

The trio flee through the ferns and cycads–Alex sure-footed in
the lead, Fletcher terrified. Rivers moves like a cat, unhurried.
Neither Rivers nor Alex glances back.

Fletcher, looking over his shoulder, stumbles. Alex hauls him
up and pulls him along. Rivers looks back...

The ROARING Terato's much closer now. Rivers CALLS
OUT:

                    RIVERS
        Meet you back at the point!

He stomps off through a shallow part of the pool–stops, and
FIRES into the air.

                    RIVERS (cont'd)
        Hey, Toro!

The Terato pursues Rivers through the pool, ROARING,
knocking vegetation aside. Smaller reptilians scatter out of its
path.

As he runs, Rivers SHOUTS back insults at the pursuing Terato.

Meanwhile, Alex drags Fletcher along, as fast as he can.

On the far side of the pool, Rivers pauses a moment to get his bearings–then alters direction slightly. A beat later, the Terato stalks in his footsteps, ROARING.

CUT TO:

EXT. SEMI-DESERT LANDSCAPE
Away from the oasis, only a few primitive shrubs grow. Nothing stirs but insects and a pair of two-foot SALTOPUS dinosaurs fighting over the carcass of a third.

An odd HUM rises–the reptiles scuttle off. There's a sudden BLURRING amid thin air–then a SHIMMER OF LIGHT, like a heat wave over asphalt. The tiny blurred speck quickly radiates outward in all directions.

The CHRONO-CUBE materializes in the blink of an eye–a metal-frame Time Machine with side-panels made of transparent plastiglass. It sits gleaming in the Sun like a high-tech elevator–and looking totally out of place.

BRUCE COHEN, the Chamber Operator, 30ish, in safari gear, breathes a SIGH of relief at his safe arrival. He looks around, sees no one–but he spies the oasis 100 feet away.

Bruce checks his futuristic-looking watch (which matches the ones worn by Rivers and Alex)–shakes his head disapprovingly.

The Terato's ROAR splits the air. Bruce looks around anxiously, hands moving instinctively to the control panel.

Suddenly, Alex and Fletcher erupt from the cycads, headed his way. Bruce's relief is palpable–he presses a key on his keyboard and the front panel opens. Alex shoves Fletcher ahead of him into the Chrono-Cube.

> BRUCE
> Where's Rivers?

Before Alex can answer, Rivers emerges on the run from the vegetation on the other side of the pool–he races to the Cube and into it.

> RIVERS
> I took the scenic route.

Bruce starts to comment, but a new ROAR drowns his words. He sees the BELLOWING Terato emerge from the cycads. He gapes.

> RIVERS (cont'd)
> Back to the future, Bruce.

> BRUCE
> You got it!

Bruce operates the keyboard–the HUMMING begins anew. Rivers and Alex aim rifles at the Terato through the closing plastiglass.

The Terato spies the Cube, ROARS, charges.

> RIVERS
> If we have to shoot through the panels, we're in trouble. Wait till the last second.

> ALEX
> What the hell do you call this?

RIVERS
The next-to-the-last second.

They hold their guns steady as the Tetaro gets ever nearer–

Now it looms above the Cube, its sharklike jaws gaping wide.

Bruce is really working the keyboard now, too scared to glance up. Rivers and Alex hold their aim steady.

The Terato's jaws clamp down around the top of the Cube. Just then, there's a SHIMMER OF LIGHT around the Cube–

–and the Terato and its world WINK OUT OF EXISTENCE! The Cube stays where it was in CENTER OF FRAME, but both Terato and arid landscape vanish, to be instantly replaced by–

INT. CHRONO-LAB #1 - DAY
The Chrono-Cube (with its passengers) now occupies the exact center of a high-tech lab. It's suspended equidistant from spherical walls above, below and on every side–as if this were the heart of a hollow steel basketball 100-feet in diameter.

What holds the Cube in place is a half-dozen energy-conducting metal spokes which lead to it from walls wholly covered by functional-looking, computeresque apparatus.

The Chrono-Cube is like a gleaming metal-and-glass spider in the center of a silvery techno-web.

SUPERIMPOSED BRIEFLY: FIVE YEARS FROM NOW

Rivers leads the way across an elevated walkway to a control ledge where PROF. GUNTHER PROCHASKA (60s) sits shutting down blinking lights on his mainframe. Alex helps

Fletcher, who's doubled over with dry heaves. Bruce looks back in disgust:

> BRUCE
> Another would-be hero upchucks all over my nice clean Chrono-Cube...

> FLETCHER
> I—want my money back. I didn't get my dinosaur—and I feel sick...

> RIVERS
> It'll pass.

> ALEX
> Time travel's a bit like being in an elevator that drops ten stories and jerks to a halt.

They reach Prochaska.

> ALEX (cont'd)
> Yo, Professor, why the long face? We've brought your precious "Wayback Machine" home safe and sound again.

> PROCHASKA
> But Bradford and Hamlin didn't.

Rivers and Alex react.

> RIVERS
> Something go wrong with their safari?

Prochaska gestures to Fletcher; this isn't for an outsider's ears. He leads all four out a thick metal door which slides into the wall. Alex hands Fletcher over to a reluctant Bruce.

INT. CORRIDOR - DAY
Outside the door (marked "1"), they face one marked "2,"
which is slightly dented, as if pushed by great forces within.
Rivers and Alex react to this, puzzled. As Bruce helps Fletcher
down the corridor toward a third metal door some yards distant, Prochaska motions Rivers and Alex to drop back.

                    PROCHASKA
          You know Bradford and Hamlin had taken three
          clients back to the Pleistocene a week ago, in
          Cube #2.

                    RIVERS
          Hunting mastodon.

                    PROCHASKA
          Rodriguez was anchoring this end. Just before they
          were due to re-materialize, he buzzed me he was
          getting weird readings from the time stream.

                    ALEX
          What kind of readings?

                    PROCHASKA
          As if the Cube were stopping in various eras, each
          time for a fraction of a second–like a rock skipping
          across a pond, and gradually slowing down–losing
          momentum.
                    (uses hand gestures)
          And then–

He uses a palm code to open #2 Door. As they enter, Rivers
and Alex exchange a glance that says: What's up?

INT. CHRONO-LAB #2 - DAY

The three men stand on a CREAKING, badly damaged ledge inside a spherical lab identical to the first, except that all hell has clearly broken loose here–and recently.

                    PROCHASKA
          Then–this.

Where a Chrono-Cube should be are only twisted shards of metal–broken spokes dangle–both mainframe and high-tech wall are in ruins–splashes of bright red spatter the walls.

                    ALEX
          My God...

The ledge sways, CREAKING ominously. Alex looks down, uneasy.

                    PROCHASKA
          They're all dead, and this is all that remains of my
          other Transporter.

                    RIVERS
          Bradford and Hamlin... I wasn't their biggest fan, but
          they didn't deserve to wind up as wallpaper.

                    PROCHASKA
          Worry about yourselves. The media's got hold of the
          story.

He exits. Rivers and Alex exchange a look. Just as they step off the swaying ledge, it collapses, CRASHING far below.

It's a feeding frenzy out there. REPORTERS & TV CREWS
jockey for position. Rivers and Alex hang back–Prochaska
steps to a mike-strewn podium as reporters SHOUT overlapping questions:

> MALE REPORTER
> Professor Prochaska, we understand there were no
> survivors...

> FEMALE REPORTER
> Is it true their remains were splattered all over the
> walls inside?

Prochaska holds up his hands for silence; the HUBBUB subsides.

> PROCHASKA
> All I can tell you right now is, There's been an acci-
> dent involving one of our licensed Time Safaris, and
> six men were killed. We suspect the cause may be a
> Time Paradox.

> MALE REPORTER
> With all due respect, Professor... what the hell's that?

> PROCHASKA
> Let's say a man travels back to a time in which he
> already exists–say, just ten years ago.

Behind him, Rivers and Alex exchange WHISPERS:

> RIVERS
> He's really gonna try to explain Time Paradox to
> these sound-bite sharks?

ALEX

He got us to understand it, didn't he?... More or less.

Prochaska goes on, like a teacher lecturing backward students.

PROCHASKA

Two versions of that man would now exist at the same time, or at least would try to–a scientific impossibility. Frankly, we fear that may be what happened today.
(off reporters' looks)
Whatever occurred, when our Time Transporter– what some insist on calling the Chrono-Cube–tried to materialize in the present, it and everyone in it were torn to bits.

More cascading QUESTIONS–then one cuts through the rest:

McMURTRIE (O.S.)

So are you finally ready to stop playing God, Professor?

Other reporters make way as SPENCER McMURTRIE (well-dressed, a bit of a dandy, 35) moves toward the mike-stand with his TV CAMERA CREW in tow. He wears a self-satisfied sneer.

Rivers and Alex grimace–Alex STAGE-WHISPERS:

ALEX

Damn! McMurtrie again!

McMurtrie stands directly below Prochaska's mike-stand.

McMURTRIE

You and your "great white hunters" are toying with
forces no one understands. And there are lots of
people–decent, God-fearing people–who demand that
you stop.

PROCHASKA

I'm glad you mentioned hunters, Mr. McMurtrie,
because I've brought along two of the best.

He steers reluctant Rivers to podium; Alex hangs back.

PROCHASKA (cont'd)

I must go initiate our investigation of this tragedy.
But Reginald Rivers of Rivers of Time, Inc. will
answer any further questions you may have.

As Prochaska ducks inside, Rivers stands ill at ease. The reporters wait for Rivers to say something. Anything.

McMURTRIE

Well, Rivers? Are you here to spoonfeed us more
gobbledygook?

RIVERS

No. Like the old song says: "And all the science
I don't understand–It's just my job, five days a
week."

This triggers a few friendly TITTERS. McMurtrie scowls.

McMURTRIE

Even when that job means risking human lives, just
so some macho fat cat can brag he shot a dinosaur?
Not just an endangered species–an extinct species!?

RIVERS

They're hardly extinct where we go. You should
come along and see. Sometimes you couldn't swing a
cat without hitting a dinosaur.
(beat; a slight smile)
Not that swinging a cat is much of a defense against a
charging Allosaur.

More LAUGHTER. Rivers has them now. As he presses on—
just beyond the media crowd, he spies:

A limo parked at the curb—two bulky BODYGUARDS
(MARV and LESTER) stand talking before the lowered rear
window. They move and we see a gorgeously gaudy
BLONDE (20s) in dark glasses eyeing Rivers non-commitally
from within. A MAN who sits beside her isn't clearly seen.

RIVERS (cont'd)

At present, Time Safaris are the only practical way to
finance Professor Prochaska's operation. His Chrono-
Cubes eat up a helluva lot of energy.

McMURTRIE

And that justifies the slaughter?

RIVERS

It's not slaughter! We kill a small, regulated quota—
and Uncle Sam gets the lion's share of our fees since
Congress passed the so-called "Tyrannosaurus Tax."
(beat)
Scientists tell us what they're learning from the
plants and animals we've brought back will help
them replace the resources lost by the burning of the
world's rain forests...

McMURTRIE

Not that you understand all that science, of course...

24

Score one for McMurtrie. The reporters wait, uncertain which to root for. Rivers glances to see how the Blonde's reacting.

The limo's gone. A Humvee driven by BO BLACK (30s), a powerfully-built African-American, pulls into its spot. Bo signals to Rivers. Rivers turns back to McMurtrie:

> RIVERS
> I don't have my own talk show, Mr. McMurtrie. I'm just one of those great white hunters you were talking about–though my partner, Alex Blackelk, is a full-blooded Sioux.

As eyes turn his way, Alex gives Rivers an I-owe-you-one look.

> RIVERS (cont'd)
> (soberly)
> Bradford and Hamlin were our competitors, but they were also our colleagues in a dangerous business. Next time it might be our turn.

McMurtrie sneers, but most of the reporters are impressed.

> ANOTHER REPORTER
> Then there'll be a "next time," despite what happened today?

> RIVERS
> Yeah. Sure. I'm a hunter. It's what I do. Now if you'll excuse me...

He and Alex push through the mob to the Humvee. Alex hops in back, Bo slides over as Rivers takes his seat and drives off.

EXT. LINDELL BOULEVARD - DAY

Rivers, tense, is driving a bit too fast. A cellphone RINGS.

                    BO
          Think this'll hurt our chances tomorrow night?

                    ALEX
          I sure as hell hope not.

                    RIVERS
               (answering phone)
          Rivers.

The VOICE on the phone is sarcastic yet friendly, female, 30s.

                    TINA (PHONE)
          I knew you'd have to answer some phone, sooner
          or later.

                    RIVERS
          Tina?

                    TINA (PHONE)
          That's right. Your ex-wife. You remember me,
          I'm in all the wedding pictures.

Rivers weaves in and out of traffic on the busy avenue as he
grows agitated. Alex and Bo exchange a nervous glance.

                    TINA (PHONE) (cont'd)
          I'm calling from L.A. I just heard about the accident
          on TV...

                    RIVERS
          And you're calling to remind me you were right?
          Time Safaris are too dangerous a way to make a
          living.

Cars HONK. Rivers, distracted, nearly rear-ends a truck before he switches lanes. Alex and Bo are pitched forward.

                    TINA (PHONE)
          It isn't about being right–or about being the strong
          silent type. But–well, I know it's been hard to keep
          your business going before, but after this–
                    (beat)
          Look, Daddy still hasn't found anybody to manage
          his ranch in Australia, and I thought maybe this
          might be the right time–

                    RIVERS
          Tina, I really appreciate this, but I'll survive.

The Humvee barely misses the door of a parked car as it's opened by a very startled DRIVER, who leaps back into it.

                    BO
                    (under his breath)
          I'm glad somebody will.

                    RIVERS
                    (into phone)
          There's a dedication party tomorrow for the zoo's
          new prehistoric exhibit. If we can keep everybody's
          minds off the fact that six people got atomized in one
          of Prochaska's Cubes 24 hours ago, we might even
          pick up a client or two.

                    TINA (PHONE)
          In other words, screw you, Tina.

Bo and Alex's eyes widen–a big-rig truck is crossing their path at an intersection ahead.

                    RIVERS
     Look, Tina.

                TINA (PHONE)
     Go to hell!

She HANGS UP. Rivers grimaces—then sees he's right on top
of the big-rig. He careens the Humvee SCREECHING past it
with inches to spare, as Alex and Bo brace for a crash.

Rivers turns calmly off onto a side street and heads for the
parking garage at the rear of a high-rise.

                    RIVERS
          What're we hurrying for?

                     BO
              (finally exhales)
          Beats hell out of me.

                                        DISSOLVE TO:

INT. CLOSE ON TV SCREEN
MTV-SPEED TV IMAGES of primeval creatures from many
eras flit by, matching the epochs as a NARRATOR reels them
off:

                NARRATOR (V.O.)
          Permian! Triassic! Jurassic! Paleocene! Rivers of
          Time, Inc., will take you to wherever—or rather,
          whenever—you want to go!

TV IMAGES of Prochaska cutting the ribbon to open the
Chrono-Center at Washington University, accompanying following V.O.:

> NARRATOR (V.O.) (cont'd)
> Less than five years ago, Nobel Prize-winning chrono-physicist Gunther Prochaska unveiled his discovery, the Time Transporter, popularly known as the Chrono-Cube.

TV: Rivers leads a safari in Kenya–Alex one in India:

> NARRATOR (V.O.) (cont'd)
> Now you can journey to the primeval world with the greatest safari guide ever to come out of Kenya, Reginald Rivers–and his partner, Alex Blackelk, who traded teaching psychology in South Dakota for stalking the jungles of India.

TV: Rivers with two camera-toting TOURISTS near a herd of Triceratops–Alex prepping a CLIENT to fire at a charging Ankylosaur–both men posing uncomfortably with three grinning "HUNTERS" by a dead Stegosaur. All the above clients are male, though of varying ages and races.

> NARRATOR (V.O.) (cont'd)
> Whether you choose a thrilling photo safari, an exciting hunting expedition or simply a breathtaking vacation that was literally undreamed-of only a few years ago, get set to–"Have the Time of Your Life"!

> RIVERS (O.S.)
> Turn that damn thing off!

INT. RIVERS OF TIME OUTER OFFICE - DAY (CONTINUOUS)
Rivers and Alex enter through glass doors reading: RIVERS OF TIME, INC. - REGINALD RIVERS & ALEXANDER BLACKELK - "HAVE THE TIME OF YOUR LIFE!" The TV is a promo monitor.

Behind a desk beneath big framed photos of dinosaurs, etc., MILLIE MINAKUCHI (50s, Asian-American Eve Arden) presses a button that kills the TV and grabs a stack of phone messages.

> MILLIE
> The phone's been ringing off the hook.

> RIVERS
> Let it ring. What do we pay you for?

Now ignoring the RINGING phone, Millie follows them into–

INT. RIVERS OF TIME - INNER OFFICE (CONTINUOUS) - DAY
A sizable birdcage sits near Rivers' desk, its door open. Photos depict Rivers and Alex in various primeval settings.

> MILLIE
> Actually, you don't. Last week's paycheck bounced.

Rivers searches for something under desks, behind drapes, etc.

> RIVERS
> Where's Cyrano got to this time?

> MILLIE
> Soon as my check clears, I'll help you look for him.

> ALEX
> Sorry about that, Millie. As it is, we'll probably have to give Fletcher a partial refund–and I guess you heard about Bradford and Hamlin?

MILLIE
(soberly)
Then it's true?

ALEX
Afraid so. So you didn't get paid last week, you
won't get paid this week, and you may not get paid
next week. If you feel that means you can't stay on,
we'll understand.

MILLIE
How can I quit? You owe me money.

Rivers and Alex smile—she likes them, despite her manner. At
his desk, Alex rifles through papers as Rivers searches for
something behind wastebaskets, mounted skulls, etc.

ALEX
Were any of the calls from potential paying custom-
ers?

MILLIE
Do you count the University? They did the usual
piss-and-moan about all the trouble they're having
raising the money for the K-T Expedition—yada,
yada, yada—
(skims the memo)
Well, the general gist was that today's "regrettable
tragedy" won't make it any easier.

ALEX
The K-T trip was always a long shot. But after today
we'll be lucky if they don't throw us off campus.

MILLIE
(skims another memo)
Oh, and a Desmond Swayzey wants to talk to you about booking a safari to the Crustacean Period.

ALEX
Cretaceous.

MILLIE
Whatever.

Alex stops shuffling papers. Rivers keeps searching.

ALEX
Did you say Desmond Swayzey?

RIVERS
Do we know him?

ALEX
Watch the news sometime. He's only the biggest lo-cal name in organized crime.
(chuckles)
Maybe he wants to take it on the lam, before the FBI finally pins something on him.

RIVERS
Well, if he does, we're not going to drive the getaway car.

MILLIE
If he's a real crook, at least maybe his check will be good.

SWAYZEY (O.S.)
It'll be good.

In the doorway stands DESMOND SWAYZEY (40s), flanked by the hulking MARV and LESTER. Alex reacts, recognizing Swayzey.

                         ALEX
          Rivers–meet Desmond Swayzey.

Rivers stops searching. Swayzey offers his hand, but Rivers manages to be on the far side of his desk. Alex pumps the hand to keep it from hanging in space. The other three exit.

                        SWAYZEY
          I think you know why I'm here.

                         RIVERS
          You're wasting your time, Mr. Swayzey. I just don't
          want you to waste ours, as well.

                         ALEX
          Maybe we shouldn't be so hasty...

                        SWAYZEY
          The Chief's got a good head on his shoulders,
          Mr. Rivers.

Alex bristles, but tries to hide it. He wants this gig.

                    SWAYZEY (cont'd)
          After today you should be glad I feel like a vacation
          someplace different.

                         RIVERS
          Why the Cretaceous?

                        SWAYZEY
          Can I be honest?

                              RIVERS
        Give it a shot.

Swayzey starts pacing around the room, looking at the photos.

                             SWAYZEY
        I don't know Cretaceous from chrysanthemums.
        I just want to bag a major dinosaur, and this guy–
                    (stops by T-Rex photo)
        Tyrannosaurus Rex–he was the biggest of 'em all,
        right? Like that "Sue," up in Chicago.

                              ALEX
        Actually, some plant-eaters grew much larger–and
        there was the Giganotosaurus, a South American
        meat-eater. But far as we know, the Rex was the big-
        gest carnosaur that ever existed in Missouri.

                             SWAYZEY
        So where does it say we have to stick to Missouri?

                              ALEX
        The Chrono-Cube only travels in time, not space. No
        matter how far back we go we always stay in exactly
        the same geographical spot we started from–though
        the scenery does change a bit.

Swayzey nods. Rivers, out of patience, sits behind his desk.

                              RIVERS
        Look, I don't intend to walk you back to the elevator,
        let alone take you and your two goons to the
        Cretaceous.

                             SWAYZEY
        Them? They're not coming. Just me and Willow.

                                34

SWAYZEY
(off their look)
She hates hunting, but maybe she can take some
snapshots or something.

Rivers gives Alex a "You-tell-him-or-I-will" look.

ALEX
I'm sorry, Mr. Swayzey, but even if we could
work everything else out–well, we generally don't–

RIVERS
We never take women on Time Safari.

WILLOW (O.S.)
Are you bullshitting me?

All four men turn at the harsh, brassy voice.

WILLOW LAMAR (the Blonde from the limo) stands in the
door in a tight-fitting dress that Swayzey would think classy,
hands on her hips *à la* Harlow. Marv and Lester look past her
at Swayzey, indicating they tried to stop her. Swayzey smirks.

SWAYZEY
Rivers, Chief... Willow Lamar.

Willow ignores Alex and strides up to face Rivers.

WILLOW
Where do you get off with that No-Girls-Allowed
crap? I could sue your ass for discrimination.

Swayzey motions Marv and Lester to leave and close the door.
As they do, he watches Willow and the hunters with amuse-
ment.

35

ALEX

Actually, Ms. Lamar, our policy's a bit more com-
plex than–

WILLOW
(in Rivers' face)
Listen, Mr. Rivers of Time, Ink–I don't really give a
rat's if I go back to Dino-World or not, but nobody
tells me I can't if Des says I can.

RIVERS

It's nothing personal. But sex can be a distraction–

WILLOW
(overlapping)
Assuming you do it right.

RIVERS

–and that's something we don't need in the middle of
the Mesozoic, so we don't go on safari with mixed
groups.

WILLOW

What, like you and normal people?

RIVERS

That's it! Both of you–out!

WILLOW

What? You're so rich? The way I hear it, any minute
they may turn this place into a parking lot.

Rivers strides to the door, tight-lipped and grim.

RIVERS

I said out!

ALEX

Now everybody just calm down. Why don't I pour us
a drink, and–

Alex strides to a slightly-ajar wall panel, and manually pivots
it so a hidden wetbar comes into view. As it does–

WHOOSH! With a SQUAWK, CYRANO THE DIMOR-
PHODON flies out as if from a starting gate, bowling Alex
over. The flying reptile has a colorful parrot-like beak and a
four-foot wingspan.

Cyrano caroms about like a trapped bat, knocking down
skulls, photos–Rivers and Alex in pursuit. When he makes a
sharp mid-air turn, Rivers trips over a chair, crashes to the
floor. Cyrano flutters down onto Willow's arm; she looks at
him.

WILLOW

Hey, he's cute.

Rivers rises, takes a fair-size conifer seed from his pocket.

RIVERS

Brought you back a treat, Cyrano. I know the Triassic's a little before your time, but...

Rivers tosses Cyrano the seed–he catches it in his beak, swallows it, SQUAWKS for more. Alex takes a step toward him.

ALEX

I told you we should've left that winged salamander
back in the primeval. Here, Ms. Lamar, I'll–

Cyrano SQUAWKS harshly at Alex, who halts. For reasons
known only to himself, Cyrano hates Alex. Rivers holds out
his arm. Cyrano looks at Willow. She nods, and he hops onto

Rivers' arm but keeps eyeing Willow, who's as colorful as he is.

                    RIVERS
          Very impressive, but this conversation is still termi-
          nated.

Willow abruptly remembers she doesn't like Rivers.

                    WILLOW
          I told you, we'll sue–

                    RIVERS
          So sue.

                    SWAYZEY
          Zip it, Willow. He knows I don't need the publicity
          of a lawsuit.

                    RIVERS
          Funny how when you turn on the light in a dark
          room, all kinds of things run for cover.

Swayzey whirls toward Rivers, glaring with a cold intensity.

                    SWAYZEY
          Don't push, Mr. Rivers. I might push back–and
          you've got no idea how hard I can push.

For the first time Rivers realizes he's in the presence of a beast
deadlier than any he's ever faced, but won't back down. Willow winks at Cyrano, leaves. Swayzey stops in the door.

                    SWAYZEY
                    (continuing)
          I always get what I want, Mr. Rivers. And I don't
          usually ask so politely.

RIVERS
Then you've had two new experiences today.

Swayzey exits behind Willow, past Marv and Lester.

INT. OUTER OFFICE - DAY
As they leave, Lester SLAMS the outer-office door, cracking the glass. Millie looks up at Rivers and Alex.

MILLIE
I take it this means I still can't cash my check?

INT. INNER OFFICE - DAY
Door closed, Alex slumps into his chair. Rivers cages Cyrano.

RIVERS
Sorry, Alex.

ALEX
You're probably right—taking a guy like that would just be asking for trouble. It's just that, ever since McMurtrie reported what our safaris cost, everybody thinks we're rolling in dough. But if we don't get some paying clients out of that shindig tomorrow, we might as well hang it up.

RIVERS
I want out, Alex. It's not fun anymore.

ALEX
You serious?

Rivers re-hangs a fallen photo of grazing Apatosaurs.

RIVERS

Maybe I should take a Chrono-Cube back to the
primeval and send it home, empty, with no
forwarding address–
     (looks out a window)
–live out my life in an era with no other human be-
ings in sight for millions of years.

ALEX

Bull! I know what you need, old buddy... and you're
not going to find it in the Mesozoic.

Rivers turns–slightly puzzled.

DISSOLVE TO:

<u>CLOSE ON KRISTEN MORGEN</u>
Mid-20s, coolly attractive in a tastefully sexy dress; she'll turn
out to have a slight European accent when she speaks. She
gazes enigmatically at the unseen Rivers across the table.

RIVERS (O.S.)

...So, Kristen, you and Andrea met in a night class at
the University?

<u>INT. UPSCALE NIGHT CLUB - NIGHT (CONTINUOUS)</u>
KRISTEN sits opposite Rivers at a table for four. Dinner's
over; an empty wine bottle sits between them. In the b.g., Alex
dances with his girl friend ANDREA (late 20s). Rivers, in a
suit, takes yet another sip of wine to hide his nervousness.

KRISTEN

Yes. I'm brushing up on my English so I can get a
good job here.

RIVERS

No class tonight?

KRISTEN
(smiles at him)
Something better came up, Reginald.

RIVERS
Rivers. I never liked "Reginald" or anything you
could make out of it, so I just go by "Rivers."

One DANCE NUMBER has ended, and another BEGINS.

KRISTEN
Would you like to dance–Rivers?

RIVERS
It's been years–

KRISTEN
And in your case that means millions of years, right?
Come on. Let's make history.

She gently but firmly leads him onto the floor. He's no Fred
Astaire, but he's no klutz, either. Alex and Andrea wave
coyly. Rivers and Kristen talk as they dance.

KRISTEN
(continuing)
Andrea told me a little about your work. It must be
exciting, like being a test pilot.

RIVERS
More like driving a schoolbus.

KRISTEN
But you're one of the first people ever to explore a
prehistoric world–

                    RIVERS
                 (stops dancing)
     You really want to know what it's like?

                    KRISTEN
     Yes. Yes, I really want to know.

                    RIVERS
     If we can find a more private spot...

                    KRISTEN
     My apartment's around the corner.

He looks back at her. Their eyes meet, lock.

                                        CUT TO:

EXT. KRISTEN'S APARTMENT BALCONY - NIGHT
Rivers and Kristen, wine glasses in hand. Rivers looks off at
the skyline. The wine has made him expansive.

                    RIVERS
     When my great-grandfather first hunted Africa, it
     was a challenge–a man with a rifle against beasts that
     dwarfed him–elephant, rhino.
                 (sighs; takes a drink)
     All that changed as the guns got bigger and the world
     got smaller. By the time Dad died, a man could bring
     down a rogue elephant from so far off he could
     barely see it without a telescopic sight. Nothing left
     for people like me to do but lead tourists around
     Kenya by the nose. Alex swears India's even worse.

                    KRISTEN
     Then along came this–Chrono-Cube?

RIVERS
(paces, sips wine)
At first it seemed like the answer. A man stalking a
carnosaur's an instant underdog. Guess I should say
"man or woman," but I've got an ironclad rule about
never taking females along. No offense meant.

KRISTEN
None taken.

RIVERS
Anyway, it didn't last. The Continental .600 rifle
came along, and suddenly anybody who can stand its
kick thinks he's Buffalo Bill.

KRISTEN
But surely there's still that element of danger that
thrilled your great-grandfather.
(hesitates)
I heard on TV about the accident. And didn't it say a
hunter was killed on the very first Time Safari three
years ago?

Rivers leans on the balcony, stares out. A painful memory.

RIVERS
Lyle Selis. My original partner. Albertosaur got him
when his first shot missed its heart.

KRISTEN
I'm sorry. I shouldn't have–

RIVERS
We accept the risks. Hell, for all I know, we need
them. But for every real tragedy, there's a dozen 30-
ton Apatosaurs that get blown away by some trigger-
happy toilet-paper tycoon–before he stops to notice

RIVERS (cont'd)

its head won't even look good over his mantle. And
even when it's some carnivore–
(beat; looks at her)
We came into their world, Kristen–they didn't invade
ours. We're the intruders.
(a deep breath)
That's why I don't want to do it anymore. I just don't
see the point.

Kristen moves in close to him, taking his glass.

KRISTEN

What will you do instead?

RIVERS

I don't know. Maybe write my memoirs. Except I'm
no writer.

KRISTEN

Perhaps I could help. There's a word processor in the
bedroom.

She sets both their glasses on the balcony railing. Staring into
each other's eyes, they gradually move nearer each other.

RIVERS

Never used one.

KRISTEN

I'll teach you. It's very user-friendly.
(lips parted)
So am I.

She kisses him. He holds back a second, then responds in
kind. One of the wine glasses is knocked off the railing–

44

ANGLE - THE WINE GLASS (SILENT)
falls, end over end, the wine spilling out in a crimson spray

EXT. THE SIDEWALK BELOW - NIGHT (SILENT)
CLOSE on the glass shattering into a million pieces on the concrete–the shattering starts in real time, then shifts to SLOW MOTION–the shards fly in all directions.

INT. CHRONO-LAB #1 - NIGHT (SILENT)
A Chrono-Cube occupies CENTER FRAME, amid the high-tech lab–then it EXPLODES IN SLOW MOTION. Metal shards tumble end over end in all directions, including directly as us.

INT. KRISTEN'S BEDROOM - DAWN
Rivers sits bolt-upright, nude in bed, waking with a sharp intake of breath. He looks around. Kristen's PC sits atop a nearby desk. He picks up a handwritten note on the pillow.

It reads: "RIVERS–SORRY I HAD TO LEAVE, BUT I HAD A DEADLINE. LOVE, KRISTEN. P.S.: WE MUST DO IT AGAIN SOMETIME!"

                    RIVERS
          Deadline?

The card in his hand begins to slowly–

                              DISSOLVE TO:

INSERT–ST. LOUIS HERALD (NEWSPAPER)
Headline: TIME MACHINE TRAGEDY AT WASHINGTON U. KILLS SIX.

Under it is a photo of Rivers at the press event near a sub-head: TIME SAFARI HUNTER WANTS TO QUIT - CALLS

MODERN MAN "INTRUDER" IN ERA OF DINOSAURS.
The byline reads: BY KRISTEN MORGEN.

Suddenly, there's the SOUND of RAPID GUNFIRE.

<u>INT. SHOOTING RANGE - DAY</u>
Rivers tosses the paper down in disgust, as Alex fires off several more accurate rounds at a target to vent his anger.

> ALEX
> My fault. Andrea and I never dreamed Kristen was a stringer, looking for something to sell to the media.

> RIVERS
> I'm a big boy, Alex. I can handle myself with dinosaurs. It's mammals I have problems with. And she was definitely a mammal.
> (grins in spite of himself; then frowns)
> This plays right into McMurtrie's hands.

> ALEX
> That's what we get for running safaris during sweeps week. Where the hell's Bo? He wanted to–

Bo enters, carrying a two-barreled rifle even bigger and more futuristic than the .600. Rivers' eyes fix on it instantly.

> BO
> Sorry. Had to climb out the back window. Damn reporters camped out on the lawn.

> ALEX
> Hey, you're weapons-modifier to the stars now, Bo.

> RIVERS
> What've you got there?

Bo hands Rivers the advanced rifle like it's the Holy Grail.

> BO
> Prototype of the Continental .1000–the only one in existence so far. You two are always bitching how our clients miss the heart...

> RIVERS
> (likes rifle's heft)
> Heart's the one place you can make a fatal hit on a big dino.

Bo pulls a switch. At the far end of the shooting range, a 6"-wide heart-shaped target appears, moving erratically.

> BO
> That's the heart of a T-Rex that's thundering right at you. The sights on this baby can seek out a heartbeat through a mountain of muscle and scales and guide the shell straight to it. Try it.

Rivers aims the .1000. Seen through the sight, the target seems small, moving randomly, but he keeps it at dead center.

> BO (O.S.)
> Don't aim too good. Remember–you're a C.E.O., not Annie Oakley!

Rivers lets the target move in and out of the crosshair, then SHOOTS a big hole in target's center. He hands Bo the rifle.

> RIVERS
> Not exactly sporting, but it might cut down on the mischief our clients can cause.

ALEX

Right. The faster they get their kill, the sooner we can bring 'em back alive.

BO
(to Rivers)
'Course, if you're planning to retire, I'm wasting my time.

RIVERS

Don't believe everything you read.

He dumps the paper into a wastebasket and heads for the door. Bo and Alex follow happy they got Rivers' adrenaline flowing.

DISSOLVE TO:

CLOSE-UP OF A SNARLING SABERTOOTH
CAMERA PULLS BACK to reveal it's in a temporary cage in a jungle habitat–atop a slightly too-small pedestal. A sign on the cage reads: EUSMILUS.

EXT. FOREST PARK ZOO, ST. LOUIS - COCKTAIL PARTY - NIGHT
Formally-attired PATRONS wander amid temporary cages holding two baby DIPLODOCUS, necks playfully entwined–a mewling TRICERATOPS calf–baby MASTODONS, DUCK-BILLS, CERATOSAURS. For mood, jungle netting hangs hammock-like above the area. Alex (in tux, with Andrea amid several patrons) is responding to a question from an over-stuffed BANKER:

ALEX

...So we haven't brought back any really large animals because we can't squeeze them into the Chrono-Cube...

ALEX (cont'd)
Most of these are very young, but don't worry, they'll
grow on you. And grow–and grow.

The "civilians" TITTER politely at Alex's little joke.

Nearby, Bo's chatting up an attractive young BLACK
WOMAN by the buffet. Both are carrying trays; Bo's is brim-
full.

BO
...I tell you, girl, you haven't lived till you've wres-
tled a ten-foot crocamander for your dinner.

WOMAN
(pokes his middle)
'Least I don't have to ask who won.

GROUPING NEAR BABY TRICERATOPS CAGE
Prochaska and Rivers (in tuxes) talk to patrons, including
mousey-looking, 45ish AUGUST & BUNNY HOLTZINGER;
the husband wears specs. Cyrano sits on Rivers' shoulder, one
leg held by a thin chain–Rivers holds the other end of the
chain and feeds him tidbits when he SQUAWKS. A 50ish
BUSINESSMAN addresses Rivers:

BUSINESSMAN
Then all your contracts give you the right to have
your clients shoot aged or dying beasts whenever
possible?

RIVERS
We figure one dinosaur head looks about as good as
another over a fireplace–or as bad, depending on your
point of view.

MRS. HOLTZINGER
That's very humane, isn't it, Augie?

Holtzinger GRUNTS, swigs a drink–he doesn't like the way his wife has been gushing over Rivers.

HOLTZINGER
Sounds to me like the dinosaurs are a lot safer than the people they take hunting.

PROCHASKA
(as several people fidget uncomfortably)
Our next expedition, which we were hoping to mount with Dr. Haupt and Dr. Featherstone here, was to have been purely scientific, but alas...

Prochaska indicates EINAR HAUPT (short, stocky) and STERLING FEATHERSTONE (tall, gangly), two 40ish men at the fringe of the group. Neither wears a tux; they're scientist types.

HAUPT
They may scrape together the rest of the money for the K-T Expedition yet, Professor.

FEATHERSTONE
Sure–soon as they find a way to televise a football game from the Late Cretaceous!

Prochaska and Rivers wince at his bitterness–Cyrano SNAPS at the Triceratops calf poking its nose through the bars.

MRS. HOLTZINGER
What's the "Katy" Expedition?

PROCHASKA
"K-T." It stands for "Cretaceous-Tertiary"–referring
to the border between two distinct geologic periods.

RIVERS
(dumbing it down)
The so-called "K-T Event" is the cut-off point between when dinosaurs ruled the Earth, and the era
when they'd ceased to exist and our ancestors got a
chance to take over.

HOLTZINGER
He means cavemen, Bunny.

RIVERS
Actually, I meant tree shrews and voles. Men, even
apes, came along–

As Holtzinger scowls and takes another swig, Rivers sees
Swayzey arrive some yards away–a flashily-dressed Willow
on his arm. Eyes turn at the arrival of the local gangster, Marv
and Lester hang back, uncomfortable in their tuxes.

RIVERS (cont'd)
–a whole lot later.

Willow's eyes meet his. She glares at him, then turns away

MRS. HOLTZINGER
I don't believe I've ever heard of this "K-T Event,"
Mr. Rivers.

FEATHERSTONE
That's because it never happened!

All react. Haupt rolls his eyes. Prochaska to "civilians":

51

PROCHASKA

I fear there's a controversy in science as to whether the dinosaurs died out by natural evolutionary processes over millions of years, or whether they were extinguished far more quickly, as a result of some natural catastrophe.

MRS. HOLTZINGER
(brightening)

Oh, yes, I did read about that. You mean that big meteor that crashed a zillion years ago!

FEATHERSTONE

If one did. But it didn't.

To offset Featherstone's testy tone, Haupt interjects:

HAUPT

And I'm just as positive that it did. Maybe that's because Sterling's a paleontologist and I'm an astronomer.

RIVERS

Well, unless we send an expedition back there, we'll never know for sure. So far we've steered well clear of the period around the K-T Event.

HOLTZINGER
(scornfully; drinking)

Why? Afraid?

PROCHASKA

If a group arrived too early, it might have to wait around for years. Too late and they'd miss the cataclysm entirely. And if they materialized right as it struck, they'd be obliterated along with the dinosaurs.

Featherstone sets down his glass so hard it breaks. He stomps off. Haupt, embarrassed, addresses the others:

                    HAUPT
     I'm afraid Dr. Featherstone takes this whole thing
     personally. He's staked his reputation on there not
     being a K-T catastrophe, and he hoped the expedition
     would vindicate him.

He moves off after Featherstone. Behind them the Triceratops calf SNAPS at Cyrano. Preoccupied, Rivers doesn't notice.

                    ANOTHER PATRON
     What would you and Mr. Blackelk do on such a
     safari, Mr. Rivers?

                    RIVERS
     Mostly we'd try to keep the big sauropods from step-
     ping on the scientists, and the carnosaurs from eating
     them.

                    PROCHASKA
     Mr. Rivers and Mr. Blackelk avoid killing dinosaurs,
     whenever possible.

                    McMURTRIE (O.S.)
     Why don't you come on my show and tell people
     about it, Rivers?

All but Rivers and Prochaska smile as a smarmy Spencer McMurtrie shoehorns himself into the group.

                    McMURTRIE
     I'm sure my viewers would love to learn about all the
     personal tastes of the great dinosaur hunter. Oh, and
     by the way–

McMurtrie steps aside and ushers Kristen in next to him. She's tastefully dressed, but uneasy at seeing Rivers.

McMURTRIE

(continuing)

–I'd like you to meet my guest on tomorrow's show: Kristen Morgen, an up-and-coming young journalist.

RIVERS

I should've known you two would find each other.

Kristen bites her lip but smiles. Prochaska kisses her hand.

PROCHASKA

I can't remain angry at anyone so lovely... not even a reporter.

KRISTEN

Thank you. I just needed a job.

(looks at Rivers)

Please believe me, I didn't enjoy embarrassing any-one.

McMURTRIE

(he's enjoying this)

Please go on, Professor Prochaska. You were waxing eloquent about the sanctity of dinosaur life, and the nobility of the big game hunter...

HOLTZINGER

(blurts out)

I want to shoot a Triceratops!

All eyes, even his wife's, turn on Holtzinger, surprised.

PROCHASKA

I beg your pardon?

HOLTZINGER

I want to shoot a Triceratops!
    (points to calf)
Like that, only bigger! A really big one!

MRS. HOLTZINGER

Really, Augie, you can barely stand to dispose of a
dead mouse! You toss them into the garbage, trap and
all.
    (as Holtzinger looks away, shamed)
You're not going hunting for anything! I never heard
of anything so ridiculous in my life.

PROCHASKA
    (plowing on)
Uh... about what you said, Mr. McMurtrie: I'm no
philosopher, but I do believe that all life is created
equal, and that man can best sanctify his own existence by respecting that of other species.

Mrs. Holtzinger impulsively APPLAUDS these words.

The sudden NOISE startles Cyrano, already nervous near the
Triceratops calf. With a SQUAWK, he flies off Rivers' shoulder. Caught off guard, Rivers drops the chain.

WIDER COCKTAIL PARTY AREA
Cyrano careens around, startling patrons, as primeval animals
thrash in their cages. Alex and Bo join Rivers chasing Cyrano,
whose loose chain dangles behind him.

Cyrano lands on a table, flies off. Alex's lunge destroys the
table, splatters food–the mess blocks Rivers' pursuit.

Cyrano comes to rest on the Sabertooth cage on its pedestal.
SNARLING, the big cat takes a swipe at the winged reptile.

As Cyrano flies off, SQUAWKING, the loose end of his chain catches on the cage bars and jerks him to a halt in mid-air.

One of the Sabertooth's talons gets tangled in the chain–and it begins to pull Cyrano toward it. SQUAWKING, Cyrano flaps his wings harder, straining to escape.

Nearby, Rivers, Bo and Alex scramble over the fallen table.

RIVERS

Cyrano!

As the Sabertooth's paw swipes at him through the bars, Cyrano SQUAWKS and beats his wings desperately. Cyrano's big and scared enough that he pulls the cage off the pedestal–

The cage crashes to the ground–its electronic lock ZZITS open–even as Cyrano finally wriggles free of the chain and flies off to a high perch. The Sabertooth is loose!

The crowd reacts in horror–women SCREAMING, everyone SHOUTING, scrambling for safety, knocking each other over. Security Guards (and Marv and Lester, who automatically reach for pistols in their jackets) can't wade through the panic.

Mrs. Holtzinger, shoved by another fleeing patron, falls into the path of the SNARLING Sabertooth–she SCREAMS. Suddenly, Rivers runs into the Sabertooth's path. He grabs a chair and holds it before him, like a lion tamer.

RIVERS

Here, Smiley! Here, kitty kitty!

The cat's paw shatters the chair. Rivers eyes the splinter in his hand, then sees Mrs. Holtzinger crawl behind a small table. He tosses the splinter at the cat; it knocks it away.

The Sabertooth's about to leap at Rivers, when it's struck by a small table, flung by Bo, yards off. It turns toward Bo.

                              BO
         Uh-oh.

Bo overturns the table behind which Mrs. Holtzinger cringes, just before the Sabertooth smashes into it, CRACKING it. Bo keeps the table between them as the cat's claws shred it.

Rivers looks up and spots the jungle netting above where the Sabertooth's attacking Bo and Mrs. Holtzinger.

ABOVE THE COCKTAIL PARTY AREA
Rivers scrambles agilely up one of the metal poles supporting the netting, but reaching the top he finds he has nothing to cut the netting with. He spies Alex hurling objects at the Sabertooth in a vain attempt to distract it from Bo.

                           RIVERS
         Alex–a knife!

Alex scoops up something we don't see clearly. In a moment, it's flashing through the air toward Rivers. Rivers catches it in one hand. It's a butter knife! He glares down at Alex.

Alex shrugs–"that was the best I could do"–and throws more items at the feline which is fast denuding Bo's defenses.

Rivers desperately saws at a not-thick wooden pole that holds up one side of the netting. He doesn't make any headway.

Below, the Sabertooth sweeps away the last splinters of Bo's table. The SCREAMING Mrs. Holtzinger cowers behind him.

A deep breath–and Rivers leaps into space toward the pole.

He reaches it—just barely—

Just as he breathes easy, his weight and momentum break the pole in two. Both halves, the net, Rivers—all hurtle down in an arc toward the cat crouched to leap at Bo and Mrs. H.

COCKTAIL PARTY AREA
The netting falls over the cat just in time to entangle its talons and prevent their turning Bo's face into spaghetti. Rivers lands hard on a table that collapses under his weight.

Bo rolls away with Mrs. Holtzinger as the cat thrashes about. Rivers and Alex wind the net several times around it. Bo runs up to help. Claws shred some netting but it holds.

A GUARD runs up with a tranquilizer gun, but can't get a good shot. Rivers grabs it from him and SHOOTS the cat. FWIP!

The Sabertooth's thrashing ceases. A paw jutting up through the net, it looks for all the world like a sleeping pussycat.

PANTING, Rivers, Alex and Bo look down at it, then at each other. Grinning spontaneously, they high-five each other.

As the crowd goes wild with APPLAUSE, Prochaska strides up with Haupt and Featherstone. McMurtrie and Kristen arrive, Kristen talking into his ear. Holtzinger rushes to his wife.

                    PROCHASKA
          Is everyone all right?

                    BO
          I will be, soon as I change my pants.

McMURTRIE

That was a defining moment–and we got it all on
tape.

He points to a TV CAMERAMAN, who had scrambled onto a
high vantage point to get the shot from a safe distance.

RIVERS

Well, that makes it all worthwhile, doesn't it?

McMURTRIE

No, but I'll tell you what will,
(raises his arms and addresses the crowd)
Ladies and gentlemen, what we've just seen is only a
small foretaste of what's to come. Because "Spencer
McMurtrie Live" is going to help finance the next
Time Safari–a scientific expedition back to "The Day
the Dinosaurs Died!"

Rivers, Alex and Prochaska look at each other, amazed.

McMURTRIE (cont'd)

And I'll be going along, to bring it all right into the
world's living-room!

People are momentarily shocked, then erupt into more AP-
PLAUSE.

RIVERS

Like hell you will! Tell him, Professor...

He turns to Prochaska–the Prof is smiling at McMurtrie.

Rivers whirls to Alex. Alex shrugs. Cyrano flutters down onto
Rivers' shoulder. McMurtrie smirks at Rivers:

McMURTRIE
You said I should go along on one of your little
jaunts, Rivers.

PROCHASKA
Your gesture is appreciated, Mr. McMurtrie. But I
fear the K-T Expedition may cost more than your
show and the University together can afford.

SWAYZEY (O.S.)
Then I'll take care of the rest.

Swayzey joins them–Willow on his arm, still breathing heavily from the excitement. Cyrano hops from Rivers' shoulder to
her bare arm. She smiles and tweaks his beak.

RIVERS
I've already told you no, Mr. Swayzey.

Willow stares. Few stand up to Swayzey once, let alone twice.

SWAYZEY
I was talking to the Professor.

RIVERS
I'll take McMurtrie if you push it, Professor. But if
you try to shove this crook off on me, I walk.

SWAYZEY
So let the Chief run the show.

ALEX
I meant to tell you before, Mr. Swayzey–I don't like
being called Chief. And Rivers speaks for us both.

Swayzey bristles. Willow looks at him anxiously.

PROCHASKA

I'm sorry. Rivers and Blackelk have final say as to whom they'll take on safari. If they say no–it's no.

Fuming, Swayzey drags Willow off. Glancing back, Willow shakes her arm gently, and Cyrano flies back to Rivers.

RIVERS

Thanks, Professor.

PROCHASKA

Don't thank me. You may just have put us both out of business. No one else is likely to come forward–

HOLTZINGER (O.S.)

I will!

Everyone whirls–to see Holtzinger standing next to his still-shaken wife. Taken aback, she starts to speak, but:

HOLTZINGER

Don't try to talk me out of it, Bunny. I'm going, and I'm not coming back without a Triceratops head. And nothing you can say will change my mind.

Mrs. Holtzinger again starts to say something, then clams up. Holtzinger gives Prochaska and the hunters a sheepish grin.

HOLTZINGER

Well. I guess that settles that.

Rivers, Alex and Prochaska exchange a "What next?" look.

WIDER ANGLE - ZOO - COCKTAIL PARTY AREA
ZOO ATTENDANTS drag off the Sabertooth–the party slowly begins anew. Rivers stands near chatting Alex, Andrea and Prochaska; he looks over at the Holtzingers talking with

well-wishers. Mrs. H. is already boasting about Augie's bravery.

Rivers notices Holtzinger looking askance at the Baby Triceratops, as it HONKS and bangs its little horns hard against its cage. Holtzinger looks a bit sickly–doubtless at the thought of an adult Triceratops charging him.

With Cyrano on his shoulder, Rivers strides out of the party, politely excusing his way past those wanting to talk to him.

DISSOLVE TO:

EXT. ST. LOUIS SKYLINE - NIGHT
The Arch and the river look as if they've been here forever, instead of existing only in a pinpoint of geological time.

INT. RIVERS' HIGHRISE APARTMENT - LIVING ROOM - NIGHT
Rivers enters. Except for a few time-travel photos this could be the pad of any unmarried male mostly interested in a place to sleep. Cyrano hops onto his perch near a window. Rivers tosses coat and tie on a sofa, heads into the bedroom.

INT. RIVERS' BEDROOM - NIGHT (CONTINUOUS)
Turning on a light, he stands before a mirror. Without looking into it, he removes his shirt. He reaches for his belt buckle, then hesitates for no particular reason.

WILLOW (O.S.)
No need to stop on my account.

As Rivers whirls, he steps aside–and we see the reflection of Willow Lamar, lounging on his bed in her sexy evening dress, smiling. Rivers instantly seethes.

RIVERS
How the hell'd you get in here?

WILLOW
Your doorman probably figured it'd do you good to
entertain a lady–after all you've been through lately.

RIVERS
Where's Swayzey? Under the bed?

WILLOW
We're not joined at the hip, y'know.

RIVERS
I didn't think that's where you were joined. Now get
out, before I call the cops.

He grabs her arm and pulls her to her feet.

WILLOW
Don't you want to find out why I came?

A beat; he lets go.

WILLOW (cont'd)
First of all, Des didn't send me. I came on my own.

Rivers looks skeptical.

WILLOW (cont'd)
Look, I don't know much about Des' business.
I don't wanna know. But he's on the level about just
wanting to bag one lousy dinosaur.

RIVERS
Tell somebody who cares.

WILLOW

He really needs some time away from–well, there's a
lot of competition in his line of work, y'know? And
you can't tell me your expedition doesn't need the
cash.

RIVERS

Somebody else came up with the money.

WILLOW

I'm bettin' you can use more. You were sayin' yes-
terday how your little safaris cost an arm and a leg.

RIVERS

You mean you were actually listening?

Willow rises on her knees, till her face is very near Rivers',
and stares into his eyes. She speaks softly:

WILLOW

I listen when I spot somebody worth listening to.

Rivers isn't certain for a moment whether to shove her or kiss
her. After a beat, he settles for turning away.

RIVERS

What do you get out of it if he goes?

WILLOW
(hesitates; then:)
Well... frankly, things haven't been so hot between
the two of us lately. I figure if he thinks I talked you
into taking him along, it might help. At least it
couldn't hurt.

This isn't the answer Rivers expected. He watches, intrigued,
as Willow strides off into the living room.

<u>INT. LIVING ROOM - NIGHT (CONTINUOUS)</u>
As they near the front door, Cyrano spots Willow, SQUAWKS and flies to her arm. She pets his beak; he loves it.

                    RIVERS
          What if I decided to go against my better judgment
          and take your boy friend? That still doesn't get you a
          ticket.

                    WILLOW
          Easy. I make plans like I'm gonna go, then on the big
          day I get sick and can't. Des won't really care. He
          just cared about you saying no to him.

Rivers weighs this.

                    WILLOW (cont'd)
          So what do you say, Rivers? We got a deal?

Suddenly, she seems soft and vulnerable behind that brassy facade. He hesitates–then, as he opens the door:

                    RIVERS
          OK. We've got a deal.

She pauses in the door, transfers Cyrano to his shoulder.

                    RIVERS (cont'd)
          By the way, if you were thinking of coming on to me
          in there, it wouldn't have worked. I've had my quota
          of seductions for this week.

> WILLOW
>
> You won't believe this, and I don't really care–but I'm only with one man at a time. If it's Des–then it's Des, and that's it.

She goes; halts in hall.

> WILLOW (cont'd)
>
> If it wasn't Des–
> > (beat; then:)
>
> But it is.

She strides off down the hall. Rivers watches her go–then closes the door and takes Cyrano to his perch. Cyrano hops on–Rivers stands petting him and gazing out the window.

EXT. STREET IN FRONT OF RIVERS' BUILDING - NIGHT

Willow strides out, pausing only to exchange a shrug and a smile with the DOORMAN. As she walks down the street, the limo we saw before pulls up. She gets in the back seat.

INT. LIMO - NIGHT

Willow sits down next to Swayzey. She doesn't look at him. Each stares straight ahead as the limo pulls away.

> DISSOLVE TO:

MONTAGE

A SERIES of quick-paced scenes (UNDER MUSIC) of preparation for the K-T Expedition–NO DIALOGUE ON SOUND:

INT. CHRONO-LAB - DAY

Prochaska and Bruce check out the Chrono-Cube.

INT. SHOOTING RANGE - DAY

Rivers helps Holtzinger aim a Continental .600. BOOM!

Firing it knocks him on his ass. Rivers sighs, helps him up.

INT. MAIN LAB (NOT CHRONO-LAB) - DAY
Bo oversees delivery of a big-screen computer combined with a state-of-the-art spectro-telescope–Haupt clucks over his apparatus–Featherstone sulks nearby, sneering.

INT. SHOOTING RANGE - DAY
Rivers and Alex try to get McMurtrie to handle a .600. He indicates his compact Ultra-Camcorder is all he means to aim.

INT. LAB KITCHEN - DAY
Alex with MING, 40ish Chinese cook, who's readying cooking equipment for the trip–excitable Ming claims he needs more.

INT. SHOOTING RANGE - DAY
Rivers with Holtzinger, who fires the .600 again. Again, it knocks him on his tail. Rivers shakes his head.

INT. CHRONO-LAB - DAY
Alex shows UNIVERSITY OFFICIALS around as Bo oversees loading by PANDRO and SANCHEZ, smallish roustabout types (late 20s).

INT. RIVERS' BEDROOM - NIGHT
Rivers sits in bed, in a robe, feeding Cyrano tidbits as the Kong/T-Rex fight from *King Kong* (B&W) plays on TV.

INT. MAIN LAB - DAY
Haupt proudly shows Rivers and Alex the finer points of the working of his spectro-telescope. They're impressed.

INT. SHOOTING RANGE - DAY
Rivers and Alex watch Holtzinger fire a .600–he's knocked down again. Rivers sighs–Alex hands Holtzinger a .500.

Swayzey and Willow enter with Marv and Lester. Rivers leaves with Holtzinger, leaving Alex to greet them. Willow notices.

INT. MAIN LAB - DAY
Featherstone and Haupt in a heated shouting-match. Prochaska walks over to calm things. Featherstone stomps off angrily.

INT. SHOOTING RANGE - DAY
Alex oversees Swayzey shooting the .1000. The kick bothers Swayzey a bit, but he can handle it–and he likes it.

INT. RIVERS' LIVING ROOM - NIGHT
Alex, Bo and Rivers watch McMurtrie's talk show–Kristen comes on to demonstrate the no-tape, solid-state portable Ultra-Cam–Rivers stalks out–Alex motions Bo, let him go.

INT. SHOOTING RANGE - DAY
Rivers practices with the .1000, to work out his frustrations.

INT. MAIN LAB - DAY
Alex with Bo near equipment being piled up, indicating the pace has got to speed up–they're down to the wire.

INT. SHOOTING RANGE - DAY
Rivers watches Holtzinger fire the .500. The kick jolts him but he doesn't fall. He beams; Rivers congratulates him.

INT. CHRONO-LAB - DAY
Haupt oversees loading equipment into the Cube. Rivers feeds Cyrano a tidbit on a perch near mainframe.

Willow enters–Cyrano flies to her, offers her the tidbit. Rivers annoyed.

INT. NIGHT CLUB - NIGHT
A final night of relaxation before the time-jump. While Alex
and Andrea dance, Rivers nurses a drink at the bar.

DISSOLVE TO:

INT. CHRONO-LAB - NIGHT
It's dark–no one around. CLOSE on the Chrono-Cube, then
CAMERA PULLS BACK to reveal the entire lab, with the
loaded Cube suspended in its metal spoke-web–waiting for
dawn.

DISSOLVE TO:

INT. MAIN LAB - DAY
Expedition members and support group mill about, talking,
most in safari garb, clearly waiting for something. Folding
chairs face Haupt's big computer with its huge monitor screen.

Rivers, Alex, Bo and Prochaska discuss a final point. Glum,
Holtzinger stands with his wife. Bruce jokes with Sanchez,
Pandro and Ming. Haupt and Featherstone talk, a bit formally.

Swayzey and Willow enter in safari garb, followed by Marv
and Lester. Willow's shirt shows cleavage. Prochaska and
Alex move to greet them–Rivers and Bo don't. Rivers mutters:

RIVERS
I thought she was sick.

BO
She looks plenty healthy to me.

Rivers moves to Willow.

RIVERS
I thought you weren't going.

                    SWAYZEY
        You know damn well she is.

                    RIVERS
                (to Willow, covering)
        Last time at the shooting range, you–looked kind-of
        under the weather.

                    WILLOW
                (shrugs nonchalantly)
        I got better.

Rivers glares at her, but Willow won't be ruffled. He turns to
stalk off, and sees Kristen, her super-mini-camcorder slung
over her shoulder, working at looking cool and collected.

As Rivers reacts, McMurtrie, all show-biz smiles, joins her–
he's on crutches, one leg in a full-length cast. He hobbles over
to Prochaska's group with Kristen in tow.

                    PROCHASKA
        What happened, Mr. McMurtrie?

                    McMURTRIE
        Hit-and-run driver clipped me last night crossing
        Forsythe. I didn't call–didn't want to upset anybody.

                    ALEX
        We can't take a man with a broken leg.

                    McMURTRIE
        Kristen's going in my place. She's now a full-time
        employee of McMurtrie, Ltd., and she's as good with
        the solid-state Ultra-Camcorder as I am.

                        70

RIVERS
(fuming; to Prochaska)
Let Holtzinger and Swayzey ante up to replace his
share. She's not going!

KRISTEN
I told you he'd never go for it, Spence. Please–let's
go.

McMurtrie looks only at Prochaska.

McMURTRIE
We've got a contract, Professor. In case you didn't
read the fine print, it says I can send a proxy if I
want.
(lets it sink in)
If Kristen doesn't go, this whole expedition stays
parked, or come Monday I'll own your so-called
Chrono-Cube.

Prochaska looks at him distastefully, but knows he's beaten.

PROCHASKA
It's your call, Rivers. You've got a contract, too.

All eyes on Rivers. Holtzinger looks half-hopeful, but clearly
the others want Rivers to give in. Rivers stalks to a window,
looks out for a long moment; then:

RIVERS
OK, let's get this show on the road.

The whole room CHEERS, though Holtzinger's are half-
hearted. Alex pats Rivers on the back heartily, and STAGE-
WHISPERS:

ALEX
From no women allowed to a pair of 'em, huh?
Hey, we'll survive.

RIVERS
Just keep both of them away from me.

PROCHASKA
I'm afraid you'll have to leave now, Mrs. Holtzinger,
as will Mr. Swayzey's associates. And you, Mr.
McMurtrie. Thank you all for coming.

McMurtrie starts to object. Kristen nudges him. He shrugs.

MRS. HOLTZINGER
(to Holtzinger)
You take care of yourself, now, Augie. I'm so proud
of you.

She gives him a peck on the cheek. McMurtrie offers her his
arm. Holtzinger, watching them go, resists chasing them. At
Swayzey's nod, Marv and Lester follow them out, close the
door.

Only Prochaska and those who will soon face the K-T Event
are left in the lab. They look at each other in silence.

DISSOLVE TO:

CLOSE-UP OF MONITOR SCREEN
An image of North America, with no writing or borders—he
indicates a single dot of light—the location of St. Louis.

PROCHASKA (O.S.)
Here's where we are.

He moves down to Mexico.

PROCHASKA (O.S.) (cont'd)
If the geologists are right, the meteor struck here, in the Yucatan Peninsula.

A dot lights up in the Yucatan, as ANGLE WIDENS to show:

INT. MAIN LAB - DAY
Prochaska holds a computer mouse. The lab is dark.

PROCHASKA (cont'd)
Of course, the geologists may be wrong, and Dr. Featherstone right–

We see reactions of sullen Featherstone, Haupt, Rivers, etc.

PROCHASKA (cont'd)
–in which case you'll encounter only primitive flora and fauna, and Mr. Swayzey and Mr. Holtzinger can bag their trophies–while others among you gather specimens, so the safari will still have a modicum of scientific value.
(smiles wanly)
However, since this is officially the K-T Expedition, let's assume for the moment the K-T Event was a very real phenomenon, and that something big struck the Earth either in 65,971,453 B.C.... or else the following year...

WILLOW
You mean you don't know?

All eyes turn to an indignant Willow. Swayzey frowns.

WILLOW (cont'd)
I heard if we land in the middle of that K-T thing, we all get french-fried. How do you know we won't?

Rivers glares over at Alex, who avoids his eyes by staring straight ahead. Prochaska smiles benignly, and nods to Haupt.

                    PROCHASKA
          Dr. Haupt, would you mind?

Haupt rises, lighted by the monitor–smiles at Willow.

                    HAUPT
          Without going into detail, my calculations have
          narrowed the K-T Event down to a corridor of
          approximately one year. We'll be going back to the
          earlier date first, so there's no danger of getting
          "french-fried."

A few titters of nervous LAUGHTER. But Willow's serious:

                    WILLOW
          And if we're too early?

                    HAUPT
          Once we arrive, my instruments should quickly
          determine the exact month, day, even hour of the
          catastrophe.

                    PROCHASKA
          At which point, you'll be transported back here, then
          quickly time-jump to a date much closer to the K-T
          Event. As far as you're concerned, you'll be away
          from the Cretaceous only a few moments. But when
          you return there, as much as a year may have passed.

Willow lets it all sink in a beat, then settles back, smiling.

                    WILLOW
                 (settling back)
          OK–got it! No problem.

Swayzey shakes his head. Rivers glances back–and sees Kristen smiling at him, mouthing the words: "Smart girl!"

Anxious to continue, Prochaska indicates the monitor screen:

> PROCHASKA
> As I was saying–this is modern-day North America. And this–

CLICKS the mouse. SUPERIMPOSED over the map is a 65,000,000 B.C. reconfiguration of land and sea masses. A DARK IRREGULAR SHAPE splits North America in two from north to south and covers much of Mexico and USA east of Texas. The St. Louis dot isn't far north and east of the dark shape; the Yucatan dot is surrounded by it.[1]

> PROCHASKA (cont'd)
> –this is the world of the Late Cretaceous, when much of what is now dry land is covered by a great sea which cuts what is now North America in two. You'll notice that sea begins not far from where we are now.
> (indicates dark shape)
> The meteor, if it's what it is, is six miles across, and traveling several times that distance every second when it hits the Yucatan.

CLICK! The monitor shows a computerized cross-section of the Earth. A round Meteor shape descends in slowed time toward the Yucatan light-dot. St. Louis' light-dot is now off-screen.

> PROCHASKA (cont'd)
> When it strikes, it's with the force of 100 million hydrogen bombs.

---

[1] See map at end of screenplay.

The Meteor hits–shock waves radiate in all directions, including back into the Meteor, flattening it out. The impact creates an expanding, incandescent crater. The Meteor vanishes, as does much of the target rock it struck.

> PROCHASKA (cont'd)
> The impact vaporizes the meteor, sending out powerful shock waves in all directions, causing earthquakes and forming a crater 25 miles wide.

Shock waves also send bright red blobs skyward. Some of these soon fall back to Earth; others pass out of view at the top of the screen.

> PROCHASKA (cont'd)
> One shock wave spews out ejecta–melted rock and solid fragments–flinging some in high trajectories up to the outer edges of the atmosphere.
> (beat)
> Next comes the fireball.

Vaporized rock, driven outward from the impact point, resembles a nuclear explosion, except that it expands equally in all directions–there's no mushroom cloud.

CLICK! The monitor image widens to show a greater cross-section of Earth. The St. Louis dot is now visible at one side of the screen. But the fireball continues to expand.

Rivers, Alex, Holtzinger, Kristen, Swayzey, Willow et al are mesmerized, to varying degrees.

> PROCHASKA (cont'd)
> The vast cloud of vaporized rock is pushed outward, in a colossal fireball far more powerful than any nuclear device ever detonated.

PROCHASKA (cont'd)
Even hundreds of miles from Ground Zero, the de-
struction of life is total. But what about this precise
spot, where you'll soon be standing in the world of
65 million years ago?

For a beat the St. Louis dot seems beyond the fireball's range.
Then bright red ejecta dots re-enter from the top of the screen
and begin to fall all about it. Each hit makes an area pulse
bright red, like some video game of Armageddon.

PROCHASKA (cont'd)
Even 2000 miles away, the ejecta particles hurled
into the upper atmosphere begin to plummet back to
Earth. As they do, they're heated up by friction with
the air, and they transmit that incandescent heat as in-
frared light.

The "sky" area of the image slowly turns to pink, then red.

PROCHASKA (cont'd)
In an instant, continent-spanning wildfires erupt all
across the western hemisphere. In minutes, the air is
blackened by thick smoke from vast fires now consuming the primeval forests.

Rivers et al watch mesmerized at this doomsday scenario.

PROCHASKA (cont'd)
And that's when the tidal wave–the tsunami–finally
hits.
        (beat; then, with an incongruous smile)
But of course, you'll all be back here long before
most of this occurs–or else you'll be dead.

At his CLICK, the house lights come on abruptly. The audi-
ence look about sheepishly, startled by the lights. A few

LAUGH nervously, others COUGH. Rivers looks at his watch.

> RIVERS
> First shift jumps in 12 minutes.

The pros stride off to last-minute tasks. The first-timers mill about, with anxious smiles, making small talk.

> DISSOLVE TO:

INT. CHRONO-LAB - DAY
In the crowded, equipment-jammed Cube, Rivers, Alex, Bruce, Pandro, Sanchez and Ming stand as if posing for a photo–Bruce's hands are poised over controls as the usual HUMMING grows. Rivers and Alex each have a .600.

A beat. Then, amid a SHIMMERING, the Cube WINKS OUT OF EXISTENCE–only the spherical lab's tech-laden walls remain.

Bo stands with his .600 near the weaponless Kristen, Haupt, Featherstone, Holtzinger, Swayzey and Willow (Cyrano on her arm). They react to the fact that the Chrono-Cube has just vanished before their eyes. Swayzey forces a smile.

> SWAYZEY
> Now you see it–now you don't.

> PROCHASKA
> It'll take them a few minutes to unload in the Creta-
> ceous–then Bruce'11 return for the rest of you.

> WILLOW
> I can't wait.

SWAYZEY
(instantly edgy)
Look, if you're getting cold feet–

WILLOW
No chance, lover.

She impulsively kisses him. Uncomfortable, he breaks away
from her embrace after a moment. The others avoid noticing.

Kristen smiles at Bo–he can't resist smiling back. She shifts
her Ultra-Cam. Bo feels the need to say something.

BO
Rivers and Alex go first, in case a hungry meat-
eater's around when the Cube arrives. Back where
we're going, it'll land on top of a hill.

Kristen nods to indicate she understands. Cyrano SQUAWKS.

DISSOLVE TO:

INT. CHRONO-LAB - DAY
Minutes later. Nothing has happened, but one can feel the tension. Prochaska eyes readings on the mainframe.

PROCHASKA
It's coming.

A HUM rises–air BLURS at the center of the spokes–a
SHIMMER of light–and the Cube materializes. Only Bruce is
inside, like a bus driver come to pick up the kids. The first-
timers expected this but it's still unnerving, as if time has
swallowed five people. Bruce breaks the eerie mood:

BRUCE
Like they say–time's a-wasting.

SWAYZEY
And time is money, huh, Professor?

Bo makes an "After you" bow to all in general. For a beat, no
one moves–then Kristen takes a deep breath, shifts her camera
and walks out to the Cube. The spell broken, Haupt and Featherstone follow–then a hesitant Holtzinger. Swayzey starts to
take Willow's arm, but she recalls that Cyrano is on it and
looks fondly at the winged reptile.

WILLOW
Time to say goodbye.
(shakes her arm; Cyrano hops to perch)
Here's looking at you, kid.

IN THE TIME-CUBE
Swayzey, his jaw set firmly, escorts Willow into the Cube,
where Bruce waits impatiently, hands poised over controls.
Willow takes up a post behind Bruce.

BRUCE
Everybody in? Then awaaaay we go...

Prochaska and Bruce operate their separate controls–the HUM
starts–Willow looks over Bruce's shoulder, intrigued.

Bruce types away at the keyboard–a sequence of keys marked
"RETURN" - "+" - "1" - "HOUR." He sees Willow watching.

BRUCE
We can't go back to exactly the same moment we
left, or–well, you heard what happened to the other
Cube.

WILLOW
Yeah.

80

                              BRUCE
        But since we were just back there, it's possible to
        pinpoint–make us pop up a half-hour after I left there.
                         (smiles up; winks)
        That way we get out of helping them set up.

Willow nods–she's nervous. The HUMMING grows–

THE CHRONO-LAB
The Cube SHIMMERS. A beat–then, as before, the Cube
stays exactly where it was in CENTER OF FRAME–but the
lab WINKS OUT OF EXISTENCE around it, to be instantly
replaced by–

EXT. THE LATE CRETACEOUS - CAMPSITE - DAY
The Chrono-Cube (with its occupants) sits in a clearing atop a
flat-topped hill–not too far downslope begins a forest of oaks
and other trees now common in North America. Shrubs grow
amid bare patches of earth–grasses have not yet evolved. A
few PTEROSAURS drift through the distant sky.

SUPERIMPOSED BRIEFLY: THE LATE CRETACEOUS

Rivers and the others turn from setting up camp.

                              ALEX
        Come on out–nobody here but us anthropoids.

Bo exits–the others take a moment to get their bearings from
the jolt of re-materialization. The world outside seems almost
familiar, like a national park–yet weren't they in the middle of
a city a few seconds ago? As he's about to step out, Holtzinger
grasps his gut.

                              BRUCE
        Bo!

                                81

Bo hustles Holtzinger over to where he can be sick in private, away from the Cube. Bruce SIGHS in relief.

Kristen moves off, sighting her Ultra-Cam. Featherstone keeps to himself as Haupt checks his precious apparatus. Swayzey strides over to Rivers and Alex–Willow follows.

> SWAYZEY
> So when do I get the .1000? Why didn't Holtzinger and I have our guns on the jump like you three?

> RIVERS
> If we touched down in the middle of some browsing hadrosaurs, I didn't want anybody panicking and blasting away through the plastiglass.

> SWAYZEY
> It'd take more than a herd of dinosaurs to panic me.

> RIVERS
> I'll remember you said that. Alex, will you give Mr. Swayzey his rifle?
> (eyes Holtzinger)
> And Mr. Holtzinger's, when he's ready?

ANOTHER PART OF CAMPSITE
Swayzey, with Willow in tow, follows Alex to an open crate containing rifles and ammo. Alex hands Swayzey the .1000.

> SWAYZEY
> How soon do we start hunting?

> ALEX
> Soon as Dr. Haupt checks out when the Meteor's due. Good chance we'll have to load up again right away and leave.

SWAYZEY
(squints at sunny sky)
I don't see anything unusual.

ALEX
If it's an asteroid, it'll be invisible to the naked eye
till a second or two before it hits, but Haupt's
instruments can spot it a long way off. If it's going to
hit in the next few days, we'll have time to look for
your Rex.

Swayzey GRUNTS, checks the .1000. Alex moves to where
Pandro and Sanchez are helping Haupt set up his apparatus.

SPECTRO-TELESCOPE CORNER OF CAMPSITE
Rivers joins Alex and Haupt as the astronomer begins operating his combined computer/spectro-telescope. Numbers flash
on the screen. Featherstone grouses nearby.

ALEX
Hope your solar batteries hold out. We can't exactly
plug your equipment into an outlet.

FEATHERSTONE
Get on with it. The sooner we end this farce, the better.

RIVERS
Any sign of anything?

HAUPT
(not looking up)
Not so far. But it may take a half hour or so to
be certain.

Rivers nods and walks off–

ANOTHER PART OF CAMPSITE

Rivers is halfway to Bo and the recovering Holtzinger, when:

> KRISTEN (O.S.)
> Can we call a truce?

Kristen, with her camera, strides up, pushing a smile. Rivers indicates the Ultra-Cam.

> RIVERS
> Is that thing grafted onto you?

> KRISTEN
> This camcorder's experimental, worth half a million dollars. If it gets damaged, I owe Spencer McMurtrie a hundred years of indentured servitude.

> RIVERS
> I'm sure you could figure a way to work it off.

> KRISTEN
> I'm not proud of what I did, Rivers, but I can't spend the rest of my life apologizing. If I do my job here well, it'll be the best thing that ever happened to Rivers of Time, Inc.–especially in light of the recent tragedy.

> RIVERS
> (beat)
> Could be.

> KRISTEN
> So can we call a truce, for as long as we're here?

Rivers starts off, then hesitates and turns back toward her.

                    RIVERS
All right–a truce. Not a peace treaty, just a cessation
of hostilties.

                    KRISTEN
          (smiles)
I guess I'll settle for that.

                    RIVERS
We'll both have to.

She watches him head for Alex and Ming in the "kitchen"
area.

"KITCHEN" AREA OF CAMPSITE
Rivers joins Bruce and Ming–the cook is waxing eloquent:

                    MING
–and someday I'll have my own restaurant–"Ming's
Mesozoic"–where I'll bill myself as "The World's
Greatest Dinosaur Cook."

                    RIVERS
But until we have to shoot a dino for our dinner,
we'll make do with the canned chicken–

BLAM! Heads turn at the SOUND of a single GUNSHOT.
Rivers and Alex rush to Bo–the others mill about, anxious.

                    ALEX
Who's not here?

                    BO
I left Swayzey near those trees–
          (looks around)
He's gone.

                      85

Rivers hurries over to Willow. She's sitting on a rock.

> RIVERS
>
> Where's Swayzey?

> WILLOW
>
> He said he had to pee. Is it OK if I let him go
> by himself?

> RIVERS
> (to Bo)
> Stay here and keep a lookout.

Rifles in hand, Rivers and Alex rush off. Bo to the others:

> BO
>
> Everything's under control, folks. One of our Teddy
> Roosevelts just has an itchy trigger finger.

But he keeps his .600 ready. Kristen stares after Rivers.

EXT. FORESTED SLOPE - DAY .
Rivers and Alex race along, as small reptiles scurry off.
BLAM! Another shot. They adjust their direction as they run.

EXT. CLEARING AT BOTTOM OF SLOPE - DAY
CLOSE ON Swayzey, grinning triumphantly–then we see–

He stands with his smoking .1000 in the center of a clearing at
the bottom of the slope–above a young ARRHINOCERA-
TOPS, ten feet long, shot through the heart. Rivers and Alex
run up.

> ALEX
>
> Are you out of your mind? You don't shoot without
> word from Rivers or me.

SWAYZEY

I shoot when and what I want to shoot.

RIVERS

That's an Arrhinoceratops. It's no good to you.

SWAYZEY

(shrugs)
I needed some target practice.

Alex crouches by the carcass, looks up at him with disgust.

ALEX

Hardly more than an infant. Do you want a medal for this butchery?

SWAYZEY

(bristles)
Now listen, chief–

Alex rises, tense–Rivers steps between them.

RIVERS

Pull another stunt like this and I'm taking your gun away for the duration.

SWAYZEY

I wouldn't try it.

Rivers' gaze is as steely as Swayzey's. It's Swayzey who blinks and looks away–and he hates Rivers for it.

At a SOUND, they whirl, and see Kristen circling, operating her Ultra-Cam. Rivers and Alex react–Swayzey smirks and strikes a hunter's pose, placing a foot atop the carcass.

                         RIVERS
          Turn that thing off.

                         KRISTEN
          Why? It's the safari's first kill.

                         RIVERS
          Do you take pictures when somebody shoots a calf?

                         KRISTEN
          Only when the calf looks like a two-ton dragon.
                    (lowers camera)
          But if it really means that much to you, I'll
          destroy the footage.
                    (presses button)
          It's gone.

                         RIVERS
                    (surprised; a beat:)
          Good. Thanks.

     Swayzey stomps over to Rivers and Kristen, Alex on his tail.

                         SWAYZEY
          What's the big deal? This thing's been dead for
          65 million years.

                         ALEX
          We never shoot anything this close to camp.
          The body'll attract predators.

                         SWAYZEY
          If one of 'em's a Rex, I can get my trophy.

RIVERS
And if two carnosaurs get into a fight over this
carcass, the loser's just liable to wander up to
our camp looking for a consolation meal.

ALEX
Still, long as the deed's done, we might as well do
a stake-out, a little higher up the slope.

Rivers ponders a moment, nods. Kristen turns to him.

KRISTEN
May I film it, if I keep out of the way and agree to
blank out any footage you don't approve?
            (at quizzical look)
Our truce, remember? I'm not your enemy, Rivers–
not unless you make me one.

Something in her voice tells him she means it. He glances at
the forest, then starts upslope. The rest strive to keep up.

EXT. THE CAMP - DAY
As the four enter the camp, Willow runs to Swayzey. All but
Haupt gather around Rivers and Alex. Rivers addresses Bo:

RIVERS
He shot a young Arrhinoceratops. If there's a Rex in
the neighborhood, it'll challenge all comers for the
carcass. We'll give it time to show, unless Dr. Haupt
says the meteor's five minutes from splashdown.

All eyes turn toward Haupt as he comes from his apparatus.

HAUPT
It's almost exactly a year away. I've pinned it down:
65,971,454 B.C., September 13, an hour after dawn.

FEATHERSTONE

Bullshit.

He stomps off a short distance to sulk. No one pays any heed

HAUPT

And it's not a meteor. It's a comet.

The others exchange glances, not sure what that portends.

HAUPT

Doesn't mean much in practical terms, except we'll
be able to see it coming from further off because of
the tail.

Alex starts herding everyone toward the Chrono-Cube.

ALEX

OK, so it's back to the 21st century–for maybe
five minutes.

SWAYZEY

What about my Rex?

RIVERS

Odds are none would've shown anyway.

SWAYZEY

If I get one now, Willow and I won't have to go back
with you to see the Big Bang.

Rivers is unmoved, but Alex seizes on this. To Bo:

ALEX

How long'll it take to load Dr. Haupt's apparatus?

                              BO
Thirty minutes tops.

                            ALEX
                         (to Rivers)
It's ten minutes to the carcass, ten minutes back.

                           RIVERS
OK, if there's a chance it'll make the return trip two
people lighter.

Swayzey sneers, enjoying his little triumph–when Holtzinger
steps up, holding his .500, his jaw set.

                        HOLTZINGER
I'm coming, too! I know what he shot is a smaller kin
of the Triceratops. I'll settle for one of those.

                          SWAYZEY
You can have the head of the one I shot, Holtzinger.
No charge.

                        HOLTZINGER
                     (he's tempted, but:)
No, I have to get one myself.
                         (to Rivers)
I won't shoot unless you say the word.

As Rivers hesitates, Swayzey strides off–Holtzinger and Alex
behind him. Rivers stalks after them, shaking his head. Bo
helps Pandro and Sanchez load Haupt's gear into the Cube.

Willow moves to Kristen, who's adjusting her camera's
shoulder strap so she can follow the hunters. Willow nods
toward a few Pterosaurs wheeling in the far sky:

WILLOW

You know, this whole scene still doesn't seem real
to me.

KRISTEN
(fixing strap)
I would think the unreal world would be the one you
have back in St. Louis.

Willow reacts, stung.

KRISTEN (cont'd)
Your whole fate is tied up with Desmond Swayzey. If
he falls, you fall. Even if he doesn't fall, you fall
sooner or later, when he gets tired of you. It's just a
matter of time.
(beat)
I pity you.

Kristen starts out of camp, pauses as Willow blurts out:

WILLOW
Don't. At least I'm with Des because I like him.
Why're you with McMurtrie? From that piece you
wrote in the paper, I'm betting you've got a history
with Rivers, too.

KRISTEN
I had to get here.

WILLOW
(she doesn't get it)
Well–so now you're here.

KRISTEN
Yes. I'm here. Now, if you'll excuse me–

Kristen moves off toward the trees. Willow calls after her:

                         WILLOW
          Hey, listen–

Kristen looks back.

                      WILLOW (cont'd)
          No hard feelings. You be careful taking your movies!

                         KRISTEN
                        (smiles)
          If I'm lucky, I'll only need one shot.

Willow returns her smile, watches Kristen stride off into the forest.

                                        DISSOLVE TO:

EXT. CLEARING AT BOTTOM OF SLOPE - DAY
Three PTERANODONS atop the calf carcass are tearing off strips–they SQUAWK and peck at each other. A ZALAMB-DALESTES (a mammal 12" long) hops rabbit-like on the ground, catching insects that flit about the carcass.

                       ALEX (O.S.)
          One of our ancestors–taking what the big boys leave
          behind. That's the best any mammal can hope for in
          the Age of Dinosaurs.

The rodent flees as Rivers, Alex, Swayzey and Holtzinger stop yards from the carcass. A Pteranodon SQUAWKS at them.

                       HOLTZINGER
                   (awed by the carcass)
          That's just a baby one?

Swayzey shoots him a look of scorn. Thick forest begins anew a hundred yards off. Rivers suddenly reacts to something...

> RIVERS
> Something's coming. Something big.

Alex nods. They herd their clients into the trees upslope and crouch, hiding–

From the trees emerges an adult ARRHINOCERATOPS, 18 feet from horn to tip of tail. The Pteranodons shift, SQUAWKING. The Arrhino SNIFFS the carcass–nudges it gently with its horn.

FOREST'S EDGE - BOTTOM OF SLOPE
Rivers and Alex exchange looks. Holtzinger suddenly comes to life. All speak in WHISPERS:

> ALEX
> Well, I'll be damned! Must be the mother...

> HOLTZINGER
> I knew my luck would change! Can I shoot it?

> SWAYZEY
> What're you asking them for? We're paying for this trip.

Holtzinger looks from Rivers to Swayzey, and back again.

> HOLTZINGER
> You're right!

He rises and moves toward the clearing, hoisting his .500.

> RIVERS
> (to Swayzey; stern)
> Stay here. This isn't your meat.

Swayzey bristles. Rivers motions Alex–the two fan out on opposite sides of Holtzinger, but Alex sticks closer to him.

<u>THE CLEARING</u>
The Arrhino SNIFFS the wind.

Rivers HISSES over to Holtzinger, some yards away:

> RIVERS
> Your gun's just powerful enough to stop an Arrhino, but only if you get a clear shot at its heart from the side. If it charges, I'll handle it.

Concentrating, Holtzinger doesn't respond as he aims his gun. The Arrhino shuffles about–presenting its flank to him. Holtzinger closes one eye–the Arrhino in his sights. His finger twitches on the trigger, relaxes, twitches again.

The Arrhino SNORTS, and shambles back toward the woods. Holtzinger lowers his rifle, and his head. Alex moves to him.

> HOLTZINGER
> It's no use. I can't do it. Bunny was right. The whole idea of me shooting a dinosaur is ludicrous.

> ALEX
> Hey, don't worry about it. You still went hunting in the Cretaceous. How many of your friends would have the courage to do that?

> HOLTZINGER
> (brightens)
> That's right, isn't it?

He looks around.

                    HOLTZINGER
          Can we–go back now?

                      ALEX
          Sure.

Just then–BLAM! A shot. They react. BLAM! A second shot,
only a moment after the first.

EDGE OF THE FOREST
Swayzey, just outside the trees, holds his smoking .1000.

THE CLEARING
Rivers SHOUTS over to him in disgust–he's much farther
from Swayzey than are Alex and Holtzinger.

                     RIVERS
          You damned idiot!

FOREST'S EDGE - KRISTEN
She peers out from behind a tree, Ultra-Cam at eye-level.
Through it she sees Rivers–her view pans from him to Alex
and Holtzinger–beyond them, the Arrhino writhes its last.

Kristen reacts to the Arrhino–recovers and aims the Ultra-
Cam–pans until the camera's sight, which has crosshairs not
unlike a rifle's, locates Swayzey–she holds on him.

She's intent, focusing–then, through the lens she sees
Swayzey point at something O.S. She follows his point–

Emerging from the woods near the dead adult Arrhino is a
TYRANNOSAURUS REX, 40 feet long.

Kristen reacts in shock, lowering her camera.

<u>THE CLEARING</u>
Alex reacts. Holtzinger gapes, his .500 slack in his hands.

Elsewhere in the clearing, Rivers stands ready with his .600, MURMURING beneath his breath:

> RIVERS
> Well, Swayzey, there's your Rex, and you've emp-
> tied both barrels. Better reload fast!

The Rex reaches the new carcass, looming above it. At a RUMBLING GROWL from the forest, it stops–turns its head.

Rivers peers in the same direction–what the hell was that?

The Rex faces the forest–and suddenly a huge shape CRASHES NOISILY out of the trees:

A GIGANOTOSAURUS–it resembles the Rex but is 25% larger–50 feet long instead of 40. The biggest carnosaur yet known.

Rivers reacts.

> RIVERS
> My God!

Some distance away, Alex too gapes, talking to the dumb-founded Holtzinger, who doesn't even hear him:

> ALEX
> That's got to be a Giganotosaurus–or something a lot
> like it. But nobody's ever found a trace of one outside
> South America.

The Giganotosaurus stalks toward the carcass and the Rex–the Rex SNARLS back. Their combined ROARS shake the Earth.

> ALEX (O.S.)
> This baby's out of even the Rex's weight class.

SNARLING, the Rex back-pedals as the Giganotosaurus stalks forward, towering five feet or more feet above it–till the Rex has backed out of sight into the woods.

The Giganotosaurus ROARS again–undisputed master of the carcass.

Some way off, Rivers is impressed by this killing machine– HISSES to Swayzey, who circles at forest's edge, reloading:

> RIVERS
> You missed your shot at Rex, Swayzey. But if you get in closer, that .1000 might bring down its big brother.

Rivers sees Swayzey suddenly lift his .1000 and sight it. Rivers reacts, horrified:

> RIVERS
> No! Not from so far away! You won't get close enough to the heart to–

A shot rings out–BLAM! Rivers whirls toward the Giganotosaurus.

The Giganotosaurus reacts, as a bullet makes a slight flesh wound on his shoulder, nowhere near the heart.

THE GIGANOTOSAURUS' POV
In BLACK-AND-WHITE, as if seen through the Giganotosaurus' eyes–Swayzey a few hundred yards away. In between,

Alex and Holtzinger can be seen at the bottom of its peripheral vision.

THE CLEARING
Rivers SHOUTS at Swayzey at the top of his lungs:

                    RIVERS
          NO!

From the forest's edge, Swayzey fires his second shot. BLAM! This shot missed. The Giganotosaurus ROARS, stalks toward Swayzey.

Past the mesmerized Holtzinger, Alex sees Swayzey at forest's edge–and realizes he and Holtzinger are directly between Swayzey and the Giganotosaurus. He shakes Holtzinger violently–

                    ALEX
          Come on! We've got to get out of here!

Rivers sees their predicament–he starts running in their direction–but he's nowhere close.

Some distance beyond Alex and Holtzinger, Swayzey's .1000 CLICKS on an empty chamber. He starts trying to reload from his cartridge belt–but he's in too much of a hurry.

The Giganotosaurus ROARS again and stalks in Swayzey's direction–taking no notice of Alex and Holtzinger in between.

Swayzey glances up–terrified by what he sees, he fumbles the cartridges–they fall to the ground–

Rivers races in the direction of his too-distant comrades–

Alex drags Holtzinger in the direction of Swayzey and the forested slope–

Swayzey drops to his knees, frantically trying to recover the dropped shells–

Rivers running–

Alex's foot catches on a root–he and Holtzinger fall, only a few yards from Swayzey–Alex strikes his head and arm on a jagged rock–he's stunned senseless–

Swayzey looks up from his knees, his gun and a shell in his limp hands–he looks up–and up–

The Giganotosaurus towers over them all like the spectre of doom, its great jaws open wide–

Holtzinger, shaken by his fall, looks up at the Giganotosaurus –reacts in fear–grabs his .500 without thinking–behind him, Swayzey just gapes–

Rivers still racing, SHOUTING, his cry swallowed up by the tread of the Giganotosaurus and its deafening ROAR–

Holtzinger fires up at the Giganoto–BLAM! A miss–

The Giganotosaurus stops in its tracks–and looks down–

Rivers stops, still some distance from the Giganotosaurus as it turns its head slightly, and fires his .600. BLAM!

His bullet digs a bloody trench in the Giganotosaurus' cheek– blood spurts.

As the Giganotosaurus ROARS in pain, Holtzinger lifts his .500–

<u>THE GIGANOTOSAURUS' POV (B&W)</u>
Holtzinger pointing his rifle up–aiming–

<u>THE CLEARING</u>
The Giganotosaurus dips its toothy head–and engulfs the top
half of Holtzinger, rifle and all.

The Giganotosaurus rears up, Holtzinger's twitching legs jutting from its maw. We hear Holtzinger's long, agonized
SCREAM.

Rivers can't fire again without fear of hitting Holtzinger, so he
races to get closer.

The Giganotosaurus stalks off toward the far woods, ROAR-
ING–Holtzinger still half-swallowed. The screaming has
stopped.

Reaching Alex, Rivers FIRES after the Giganotosaurus–then
tosses his rifle down, grabs the big Sioux's fallen .600, and
FIRES both barrels at the Giganotosaurus' back–not much to
lose now–but it's already vanishing into the trees downslope.

Rivers examines Alex–Alex GROANS–he's coming around.

Rivers reloads his own .600 as Alex sits up. His head's only
scratched, but he grips one arm.

ALEX
Holtzinger...?

RIVERS
That thing got him.

This galvanizes Alex. Rising, Rivers looks behind them. Swayzey is crouched on his knees, shaking with fear, SOBBING.

> RIVERS
> Leave him. We've got to go after Holtzinger.

Alex tries to reload, but the pain in his arm slows him.

> RIVERS
> I'll go after him. You take Swayzey back to camp.

Before Alex can object, Rivers rushes off across the clearing toward the woods where the Giganotosaurus disappeared. Alex watches him go, then turns toward Swayzey, disgusted– as Kristen comes running toward them from the forest.

EXT. FOREST - DAY
Rivers plunges fearlessly through vines and shrubs. After several seconds, he pauses, listens–hears the SOUND of the Giganotosaurus tearing through the trees, already receding.

He rushes in that direction, but the SOUND continues to FADE–soon he can no longer hear the retreating carnosaur. But he keeps going–determined.

EXT. FOREST - AERIAL VIEW - DAY
Beneath the afternoon Sun and a few wheeling Pterosaurs, the forest primeval looks vast and endless.

> DISSOLVE TO:

EXT. CAMPSITE - DAY (SUNSET)
Long shadows stripe the clearing. The party wait anxiously for Rivers near the fully-loaded Cube. Alex, sprained arm in a sling, sits talking somberly with the others.

Willow comforts the still-shaken Swayzey, who sits reloading the .1000. He rises, shakes off her arm and snarls at Alex:

                    SWAYZEY
        It's been three hours! How much longer do we have
        to wait before we can clear out of here?

                    WILLOW
    Des, honey–

                    SWAYZEY
            (fiercely)
        Shut your mouth! This is between me and the Chief!

Willow stiffens. She knows what that tone can mean for her.

                    HAUPT
        Mr. Swayzey, we always knew we might be here at
        least a few days...

                    SWAYZEY
        If I want any shit out of you, I'll squeeze your head.

Haupt recoils. Bo rises, grim–Alex places a restraining hand
on his arm. Bo takes a breath and looks down at Alex.

                    BO
        I could go looking for him...

                    ALEX
        And who'd go looking for you? If he's alive, he'll
        find his way back, with or without Holtzinger.

Swayzey is in Alex's face now. Bo clenches his fists.

                    SWAYZEY
        Holtzinger's dead! That thing ate him–nearly ate me!

RIVERS (O.S.)
Too bad it didn't!

Heads turn as Rivers strides in, his .600 braced against his collarbone. Though somewhat the worse for wear, clothes torn by shrubs, he's every inch the hero. But his face wears a tragic look–for he's alone. He puts down his gun.

Rivers and Alex exchange a glance. Rivers shakes his head. Willow instinctively starts toward him, then catches herself, as the others crowd around Rivers, expressing their relief.

Rivers looks past the others and sees Kristen, hanging back at the outer fringe of the group. She smiles tentatively, as if uncertain he'd want her to welcome him. He smiles back.

Swayzey roils angrily at the group surrounding Rivers.

SWAYZEY
That's right, welcome him back–like he's some conquering hero, instead of the man responsible for Holtzinger's death!
(all eyes on him now)
You let him go out there with a gun that wouldn't stop a Rex, let alone that Super-Rex or whatever it was.

BO
You know damn well Holtzinger couldn't handle a .600. He wasn't supposed to have to fire at anything bigger than a Triceratops.

ALEX
If you hadn't fired, that thing would've settled for a carcass. You're the one killed Holtzinger–sure as if you put a bullet in him.

ALEX (cont'd)
(beat)
But I don't imagine he's the first man you've
had killed.

Swayzey takes a step toward Alex, fists clenched–Alex is
ready to fight despite his sling. Rivers grabs Alex's good arm–
Willow steps in front of Swayzey, pleads with him:

WILLOW
Don't–please. For me. Just this once.

RIVERS
Get your boy friend on board the Cube.

Willow tries to steer Swayzey with a forced light tone.

WILLOW
C'mon, Des, we're going home. Let's forget all this
dinosaur stuff and stick to one century from now on.

SWAYZEY
I told you to shut up!

Swayzey shoves her roughly to the ground. Next moment, he's
spun around by a strong hand on his shoulder–

–and Rivers slugs him hard in the jaw. Swayzey goes down.
Rivers looks down with disgust at the sprawled crime boss.

RIVERS
Do your two goons help you beat up women, too?

SWAYZEY
I don't need them for this.

He wades in, getting in a left to Rivers' jaw. Rivers is staggered, but rebounds with a blow sending Swayzey against the Chrono-Cube. Bruce is horrified.

                    BRUCE
        Not the Cube!

                    RIVERS
        Sorry.

Swayzey tackles Rivers—on the ground, they roll over and over, raining savage blows on each other.

Alex and Bo look for an opening, but the two-man battle is too fast and furious for them to intervene.

As Rivers and Swayzey struggle to get up, still fighting, one of Rivers' punches knocks Swayzey to the ground again—he lands near his .1000. Swayzey grabs the rifle and, still on his knees, points it at Rivers. Everyone freezes.

                    RIVERS
        Don't be a fool!

                    ALEX
        You'd have to kill all of us to get away with it, and
        then you'd never be able to operate the Cube.

                    SWAYZEY
        Oh, I'm sure that, with a little persuading, Brucie-boy
        will show me—before he gets eaten by a Rex, like the
        rest of you did.

Rivers looks for an opening. Alex and Bo exchange a glance—then each takes a step sideways, to present Swayzey with targets as far apart as possible to either side.

WILLOW
Des–don't be crazy–

She takes a step toward Swayzey–he swings the gun slightly toward her. She stops cold–astonished.

SWAYZEY
Sorry, baby, but you wouldn't add much to my alibi, and I could never be sure you wouldn't talk someday.

Swayzey spies Kristen off to one side. He nods toward Alex's and Bo's .600s, left behind when they greeted Rivers.

SWAYZEY
Kick those rifles over here.

Kristen does as ordered–the camera strap over her shoulder falls to her elbow as she complies.

RIVERS
Come to your senses, Swayzey. It's still not too late.

SWAYZEY
It's never too late, when you've got a time machine. You first...

Swayzey's finger is tensing on the trigger–Kristen swings her camera full in his face–his SHOT goes wild–

Rivers tackles Swayzey–both men go crashing into the Chrono-Cube again. It rocks slighty. Bruce winces.

Swayzey throws a roundhouse. Rivers ducks, and unleashes an uppercut–it lays Swayzey out, semi-conscious, GROAN-ING, at Willow's feet. She looks down but makes no move to help him.

Bo grabs Swayzey and hauls him roughly to his feet.

BO
TKO, bubba.

RIVERS
OK, everybody, show's over. Time to go home.

The tension broken, all head for the Cube–Bruce is already checking it out. Rivers retrieves the fallen .1000.

Haupt, Featherstone, Pandro, Sanchez and Ming join Bruce in the Cube. Bo keeps a grip on the groggy Swayzey. Alex moves to Willow, who stands looking down like a lost child.

ALEX
We can squeeze you on this jump, if you want.

WILLOW
(shakes her head)
I came with Des–I'll go back with him. After that–

She looks off–clearly she's no idea what comes after that.

Alex nods to Bruce. Bruce does his thing–the Cube HUMS, SHIMMERS–and WINKS OUT OF EXISTENCE. Pandro and Sanchez go off to have a smoke. The others stand around, waiting.

EDGE OF CAMPSITE
Rivers gazes as if trying to see beyond the trees, and doesn't turn as Kristen joins him, camera over her shoulder.

RIVERS
I never lost a client before.

KRISTEN

What about your old partner–Selis?

RIVERS

Holtzinger was an amateur. He was my responsibil-
ity, and I let him get killed.
    (beat; glances at her)
That was brave what you did.

KRISTEN

What'll you do with Swayzey while we make the
jump back here?

RIVERS

He stays with us till this safari's over.

KRISTEN
    (reacts)
You're going to bring him back here with us?
He tried to kill us–

RIVERS

Yeah, 65 million years before English Common Law,
let alone Court-TV. Alex figures if we tried to prose-
cute, a clever lawyer could argue the statute of limi-
tations works forward as well as backward.
    (shrugs)
I just want to get this over with.

KRISTEN
    (smiles)
"It's just your job, five days a week," huh?
    (as Rivers finally turns to face her)
I saw a tape of the press conference where you
quoted Elton John.

Her light remark reminds Rivers of a bitter memory:

RIVERS

Yeah, I guess McMurtrie would show that to his new protegée.

KRISTEN
(hurt in her eyes)
For what it's worth, there's nothing between McMurtrie and me.

RIVERS

Just the great bond of journalistic brotherhood, huh?

Kristen won't be put off. She moves nearer to him.

KRISTEN

That night meant something to me, Rivers. It took me a while to realize it, but ever since, I've looked for a chance to tell you. Not that you'd have listened...

RIVERS

No.

KRISTEN

I'm going to use my footage to try to make it up to you–by making the whole world realize how wonderful, how important, time safaris can be.

Rivers is puzzled by her strongly-expressed feelings, but:

RIVERS

Won't McMurtrie have something to say about that?

KRISTEN

If he doesn't tell the story the way I want it told, I'll quit and go on rival talk shows. He'll settle for the

KRISTEN (cont'd)
money and the good publicity. In two months people
will think he invented the Chrono-Cube.

RIVERS
And what do you get out of it?

She looks into his eyes as intently as on that first night.

KRISTEN
I'm smitten, Rivers. It's as simple as that.
(beat)
Or maybe not so simple.

Rivers looks at her–then takes her in his arms and kisses her.
She responds. From some yards off, Willow stares at them, her
face a mask.

Rivers and Kristen break off their kiss. Rivers looks at her.

RIVERS
Guess I should've known, when you slammed
Swayzey with your precious camera.

KRISTEN
Some risks you just have to take.

Another kiss–a deeper one, picking up where they left off a
few days back. It lasts several seconds, before:

ALEX (O.S.)
Cube's coming back!

Rivers and Kristen break their clinch and look into each
other's eyes–a new bond exists between them. They walk back
toward the others, his arm around her shoulder.

CAMPSITE

Alex watches them come–he knows what's happened. Bo keeps his grip on Swayzey. Pandro and Sanchez stub out their cigs. Willow faces away from everyone–very much alone.

HUM rises–air BLURS–light SHIMMERS–the Cube appears. Besides Haupt's equipment and minimal supplies, only Bruce is in it, trying to be jocular by imitating a railroad conductor.

                    BRUCE
          All abooooard!

Bo takes Swayzey's arm–Swayzey shakes off his hand and steps aboard. Bo, Pandro and Sanchez follow. Willow throws her head back, as proudly as she can under the circumstances, and enters–she and Swayzey don't look at each other.

Alex boards, then Rivers and Kristen. Bruce smiles at Rivers:

                    BRUCE
          Go on, say it.

                    RIVERS
               (forces a smile)
          Back to the future, Bruce.

                    BRUCE
               (loves the ritual)
          You got it!

The HUM–the SHIMMER of light–and again the Chrono-Cube (with occupants) stays where it is, in CENTER OF FRAME, but again everything else WINKS OUT OF EXIS-TENCE, to be replaced by–

112

INT. CHRONO-LAB - DAY
The Cube (with occupants) is suspended amid metal spokes. Prochaska sits operating the mainframe controls. Haupt, Featherstone, Ming, Pandro and Sanchez stand nearby. Cyrano SQUAWKS from his perch near the mainframe.

Rivers, Kristen and Alex step out–the others follow, till only Bruce, Swayzey and Bo remain in the Cube. Swayzey starts out–Bo stops him. Swayzey glares at him.

                    BO
          You just stay put, Mr. Swayzey. They won't be a mi-
          nute.

                    SWAYZEY
          Don't be a jerk! I'm outta here!

He starts forward again. Bo stops him, less gently–smiles.

                    BO
          Like I said, they won't be a minute.

Swayzey bristles, but bows to the inevitable.

ON MAINFRAME LEDGE
The group mill about. Kristen wanders off. Rivers and Alex go to Prochaska, busy at his controls. Willow waits nearby.

                    RIVERS
          With that arm you ought to stay here.

                    ALEX
          I can pull my weight, long as somebody else handles
          the .1000.

PROCHASKA

I was sorry to hear what happened. Who's going to tell Holtzinger's wife?

ALEX

I will.

RIVERS

No. I made the final decision he could go.

Alex acquiesces.

RIVERS (cont'd)

I'll go see her soon as we get back. Till then, nobody sets foot outside this building. I don't want her hearing any rumors. We owe her that much.

Alex nods. Prochaska indicates Willow–she's feeding Cyrano. Prochaska's gesture indicates: "What about her?" Rivers and Alex move to Willow. Alex speaks softly:

ALEX

Will you be OK?

WILLOW

Serves me right for thinking I really meant anything to him.
            (looks at them)
It's the rest of you better watch your back, especially you, Rivers. The last guy decked Des was his dad, and I never really believed the old man's car went off a cliff by itself.

RIVERS

We'll worry about that when we worry about it. So where'll you go now?

                    WILLOW
     Me? I'm going with you–back to Alley Oop land.
               (they react)
     Listen, if I step out on that street right now, Marv and
     Lester'll be all over me like a cheap fur. And once
     they make me tell what happened, they'll force the
     Prof to bring you back so they can free Des–and
     make this place have another bad accident.

Rivers and Alex share a look. They know she's not kidding.

                    RIVERS
     So you stay here with Professor Prochaska.

Willow indicates Kristen, checking her Ultra-Cam nearby.

                    WILLOW
     If Lois Lane can go, so can I. Des already paid my
     freight, right?

                    ALEX
     She's got a point.

Rivers throws up his hands, moves off. He can't fight them
both. Willow and Alex exchange smiles.

                    WILLOW
     Thanks. I'm sorry Des kept calling you Chief.

                    ALEX
     I've been called worse.

                    WILLOW
     Haven't we all?

                    PROCHASKA (O.S.)
     Everybody back on board!

Prochaska's call pulls them all back to reality.

THE CHRONO-LAB
Haupt and glum Featherstone have already joined Bruce, Bo and a sullen Swayzey. Willow pets the SQUAWKING Cyrano.

> WILLOW
> Here's lookin' at you again, kid.

Willow enters the Cube without looking at Swayzey. Kristen joins Rivers and Alex on the walkway. She sees Ming, Pandro and Sanchez waving from the ledge–reacts, puzzled.

> ALEX
> We want to be able to get everybody in the Cube at one time for a fast getaway, so we're just taking a few supplies and Haupt's equipment.

> KRISTEN
> (hoists camera)
> And my Ultra-Cam.

> RIVERS
> (grins)
> And your Ultra-Cam.

They join the others in the Cube–Kristen, next to Willow, smiles at her. Willow smiles back wanly.

THE CHRONO-CUBE
As Bo holds Swayzey, Alex slips handcuffs on the crime boss. Swayzey glares with hatred as Alex puts the keys in his pocket. The Cube door-panel is still ajar.

PROCHASKA
Set coordinates, Mr. Cohen.

BRUCE
All set, Prof. Prochaska.

LIGHTS FLASH on the mainframe and in the Cube. HUM-
MING begins

PROCHASKA
Next stop–the K-T Event. And may God protect
you all!

Willow stands looking over Bruce's shoulder, still intrigued in
his working of the keyboard. Bruce suddenly becomes aware
the door-panel is still partly open and reaches toward it–

Just then, Cyrano emits a SQUAWK and streaks from his
perch into the Cube–landing on the startled Willow's arm.
Even as those in the Cube react–and Bruce pulls the door
shut–

–there's the usual momentary SHIMMER OF LIGHT around
the Chrono-Cube in CENTER OF FRAME–and the entire lab
again WINKS OUT OF EXISTENCE, to be replaced by–

EXT. THE LATE CRETACEOUS - FORMER CAMPSITE -
NIGHT
The Cube (with occupants) again sits in the campsite area,
except a year has passed here since it left. The scene looks
much the same, but no trace remains of human occupation.
We don't yet see the sky, but the campsite is lit as if by a full
Moon.

FEATHERSTONE
Night landing?

                          BRUCE
         No reason why not.

                         WILLOW
                    (looks at campsite)
         You sure it's been a year? We didn't accidentally
         come back the same day?

                          BRUCE
                     (shakes his head)
         To be exact–it's been 357 days.

Rivers and Alex step out first, alert for predators. Alex hefts
his .600 awkwardly. Bo nudges the surly Swayzey out.

Willow's the last to step out, chucking Cyrano's chin and not
looking where she's walking–she bumps into Haupt's back.

                         WILLOW
         Sorry, Doc.

No response. She sees that he and all the others are staring
ahead and up at something. She follows their gaze–

Above them, the broad expanse of the heavens is lit by a long
shimmering COMET, its brilliant tail splashed across half the
sky, making things even brighter than a full-Moon night.

Nine humans and a Chrono-Cube seem very small between the
primeval forest and the vastness of the comet-streaked sky.

                         WILLOW
         Yeah, I guess this is the place, all right.

                                        DISSOLVE TO:

<u>EXT. CAMPSITE - NIGHT</u>
Alex, Featherstone and Willow (with Cyrano) watch as Rivers, Bo, Haupt and Bruce struggle lifting the large computer/spectro-telescope unit out of the Cube–it can barely be handled by all four, one on each side. Alex rubs his sprained arm. Kristen circles, filming the unloading.

The night's brightness very gradually increases, as the comet looms ever slightly larger–all the while it moves at undetectable speed down toward the southeastern horizon.

Swayzey is handcuffed to a thick shrub at center of camp.

                    SWAYZEY
               (jerks at his cuffs)
          Hey, what if a dinosaur comes sniffing around?

                      BO
          If we can stand the smell, he can take his chances
          like the rest of us.

Haupt and Bruce are both having trouble holding up their sides of the apparatus.

                    BRUCE
          It's slipping–

Alex moves to Bruce side, and with his good arm the two of them can just handle his side–

But Haupt's side is still slipping. He GRUNTS–everyone sees what's happening, but no one can shift his position.

Haupt looks at Featherstone–Featherstone holds back; he can't bring himelf to help Haupt.

Willow puts Cyrano down and rushes to help Haupt. She's game–and just quite strong enough. Their side holds.

The group ease the apparatus to the ground and breathe easier. Featherstone moves away. Kristen's still shooting.

                                        DISSOLVE TO:

EXT. CAMPSITE - NIGHT
A short time later. As Haupt operates his apparatus and others perform various tasks, Rivers moves to where Willow is feeding Cyrano a tidbit–she's glad to have something to do.

                    RIVERS
          I won't have time to watch him, so that'll be your job
          till we go back.

                    WILLOW
          That's fine by me. We're buddies, aren't we, Cyrano?

She nudges Cyrano under his beak–he SQUAWKS contentedly.

                    RIVERS
          Funny how he just took to you.

                    WILLOW
          It happens that way sometimes. Happens the
          opposite, too.
                    (beat)
          Are we really close to the sea?

Rivers takes Cyrano and motions her to follow him.

He leads her to a more secluded angle, and gestures toward a better vantage point of the southeast horizon below the Comet.

RIVERS

Prochaska says this area was actually underwater for part the Cretaceous. But right now the sea is 30 miles to the south, out there somewhere. Anyway, I'd better–

(starts off; turns)

How did you wind up with a man like Swayzey?

She shrugs, looks off into the primeval.

WILLOW

I'm not like you–I've never had the option of not looking out for number one.

(beat)

No, it's more than that. I've stayed with Des because he was the one who wanted me for more than a little while. And he was good to me–well, most of the time.

(touches her cheek)

It's been a long time since I was sure I'd exist if he wasn't in my life.

RIVERS

Sorry. None of my business.

He starts to leave again. He stops when she blurts out:

WILLOW

Des said you were married.

RIVERS

A few years back. It didn't work out.

WILLOW

(good-naturedly)

What happened? She didn't like your "no-girls-allowed" rule?

With released feeling, Rivers gestures toward the horizon.

> RIVERS
> Look at this place. Even with the spectre of death
> looming over it–no video, no trophy head could ever
> capture the wildness of it–the sheer beauty of it.

Willow stands transfixed by the emotion pouring out of him.

> WILLOW
> (looks around)
> Yeah, I've got to admit–it does kind of get to you.

As they talk, they wander downslope toward the forest's edge.

> RIVERS
> I brought Tina to the Mezosoic once. My wedding
> present to her. A whole world, spread out at her feet
> like Eden–though admittedly there was a serpent or
> two around. As it turned out, the most dangerous
> thing we ran into was Cyrano, barely out of the shell–

He clucks Cyrano under the beak, lets him hop onto a log–
then he looks out toward the forest.

> RIVERS (cont'd)
> But she still couldn't wait to get out. And after that,
> she spent the whole year of our marriage trying to get
> me to quit going on Time Safaris.

Neither notices as Cyrano spots a baby STENONYCHO-
SAURUS, only a few inches tall and walking on two legs, at
forest's edge–he hops off his perch after it. The tiny Steno
scampers off into the woods, and Cyrano hops (not flies) after
it.

Rivers is still lost in his own thoughts.

> RIVERS (cont'd)
> In the end she left. Funny thing is, she hated the pri-
> meval, but when she went away, she took it with her–
> the joy I felt in all those countless Edens. Since then
> it's been–a job.

EXT. THE FOREST – NIGHT
Cyrano hops in short hops after the baby Steno, which always
stays just ahead of him–leading him deeper into the woods.

EXT. FOREST'S EDGE - NIGHT
Rivers turns back toward Willow, who's gazing at him intently.

> RIVERS
> So who am I to pass judgment on what other people
> do to be happy, or even just to survive? I used to
> think I'd get over her in the end because I had time–
> all the time in the world. But maybe time isn't
> enough.
> WILLOW
> I hope Kristen brings back some of that joy for you,
> Rivers. I really mean that.

They look at each other across an unbreachable gap.

> SWAYZEY (O.S.)
> Hey, you got no right to take pictures of me!

Rivers and Willow turn back toward the campsite.

EXT. CAMPSITE - NIGHT (CONTINUOUS)
Swayzey is snarling at Kirsten, who stands aiming her Ultra-
Cam at him–she lowers it and smiles enigmatically.

KRISTEN

I wasn't going to.

Rivers joins Kristen. Willow stops at the edge of camp, turns away. Kristen to Rivers:

KRISTEN (cont'd)

But he does make a sight, doesn't he? The crime kingpin of the Midwest, all trussed up like a pig for slaughter, no bodyguards around to protect him.

RIVERS

Yeah, I imagine the FBI would like to see him that way.

KRISTEN

Maybe a few others, as well.

Swayzey turns away, sullen. Haupt and Alex stride up, with Bo and Bruce in tow. Featherstone hangs back. Haupt is carrying long tube-like apparatus from his 'scope.

HAUPT

The Comet will strike about an hour after dawn.
(indicates tube)
Anybody got an oil can?

KRISTEN

(looks at her watch)
What time will that be, Dr. Haupt?

RIVERS

Doesn't work that way. Back here the Earth rotates about once every 20 hours, so we can't use a 24-hour system.

HAUPT
(to Kristen, helpful)
It's just over seven hours... till doomsday.

He moves back toward his apparatus. The others watch him go.

EXT. NEAR FOREST'S EDGE - NIGHT
Willow has wandered off to be by herself beneath the looming Comet. Spotting the log where Rivers desposited Cyrano, she suddenly realizes he's gone. She looks toward the forest–

WILLOW
Cyrano?

She moves to the forest–and into it.

EXT. THE FOREST - NIGHT
Cyrano hops after the elusive baby Steno. When it hops into a clumpet of bushes, he hops in after him.

Willow has seen this, and moves to the bushes, calling softly. She's uneasy being here, even on a bright night.

WILLOW
Cyrano...

Willow spots him atop something half-hidden that resembles a big thorn–pecking at it. She approaches slowly, reaches forward–just as Cyrano spots the tiny Steno again nearby–

WILLOW
Gotcha!

Just as she grabs for him, Cyrano flies off after the tiny Steno– and Willow grabs hold of the thorn-like object.

She's lifted into the air as a 20 feet-long ANKYLOSAUR raises its head–she has grabbed one of the spikes on its armored head.

The Ankylosaur HONKS–shakes its head. Willow lets go, falling to the ground.

She's up like a shot, ready to flee, but the Ankylosaur is already lumbering off, having no interest in Willow.

Exhaling, Willow looks around for Cyrano. The baby Steno dangles by its tail from his beak, making little SCREECHES.

Willow starts toward Cyrano and his prize, but halts, as–

An adult Stenonychosaurus–6 feet long, though standing only about 4 feet tall and looking like a reptilian version of an emu–hops from the bushes.

Startled, Cyrano drops the baby Steno and flies off.

                    WILLOW
         Want the kid, huh? OK, mom, he's all yours.

But now another adult Steno hops out of the bushes–then another–till there are half a dozen of them.

They want Cyrano, who flies to Willow–Stenos eat small animals. Willow assumes they want her, and flees SCREAMING–Cyrano flying just ahead of her. The Stenos give chase.

EXT. CAMPSITE - NIGHT
Her SCREAM reverberates in the camp–all whirl toward it.

                    RIVERS
         Willow!

Rivers starts to go after her–but he doesn't have to.

Willow runs into camp, Cyrano flying above her–the pursuing Stenos not far behind. Bo grabs his rifle, but can't get off a clear shot without endangering Willow.

Rivers tackles Willow and they roll out of the path of the Stenos, who keep on–after flying, SQUAWKING Cyrano.

> RIVERS
> They're after Cyrano, not Willow! No need to shoot!

Bo turns his .600, grasping it by the butt. Cyrano swoops past his head, a Steno in hot pursuit. Bo hits the Steno in the shoulder–it SCREECHES and runs back toward the woods.

> BO
> They're just a bunch of big chickens!

> ALEX
> C'mon, they'll run if we stand up to them!

Now, as the Stenos run through the camp, the other members of the expedition get into the mood of things. They pick up whatever lies at hand and meet the Stenos.

With his good arm, Alex punches one in the long-beaked snout it sticks in his face. It goes down, recovers and runs off.

Haupt swings his tube–it misses a Steno, which races off toward the woods–only then does Haupt realize he could have damaged a valuable piece of equipment.

As a Steno chases Cyrano toward Kristen, she raises her camera and sights through it–but Cyrano veers off, as does the Steno.

SQUAWKING, Cyrano flies erratically through camp, only a couple of the Stenos still in single-minded pursuit.

Swayzey, handcuffed to the shrub, huddles up to prevent a small target as the two Stenos race by him after Cyrano.

Alex and Bruce form a flying block to shield the Cube. The Stenos halt as the two men charge, and flee to the woods—knocking Featherstone on his tail as they go—he's not hurt.

The Stenos are gone, and for a moment all is quiet in camp.

Cyrano flutters down again to rest on Willow's shoulder, where she stands with Rivers, who holds his .1000 by the butt.

At this, Bo starts to LAUGH—then Alex and Bruce—then Rivers and Willow—partly in relief, partly because it's just plain funny—even Featherstone, sprawled on his ass, LAUGHS—till everyone in camp is doubled over with LAUGHTER.

When the LAUGHTER finally fades, Willow turns to Rivers:

                    WILLOW
I'm sorry. I was supposed to keep an eye on Cyrano.

                    RIVERS
My fault. I had him last. You're lucky you didn't run into anything bigger than those Stenos.

                    WILLOW
         (starts to say more, then stops)
Yeah.

                    ALEX
Well, that's enough excitement for the last evening of the Late Great Cretaceous.

Haupt stretches, YAWNS. Rivers notices, nods to Alex.

                    ALEX
        We should have a bite to eat and get some rest.
        Too dangerous to go wandering around in the
        dark.

                    WILLOW
        Tell me about it.

She starts to say more to Rivers–but Kristen approaches,
holding a knapsack. Willow moves off with Cyrano. Everyone
but Swayzey mills about, talking and chuckling, in a good
mood–but Featherstone has to get up by himself.

Kristen holds up a bottle of champagne from her knapsack.

                    KRISTEN
        Anyone care for a bit of champagne with dinner?
        It's not chilled, but–

                    HAUPT
                (responds happily)
        I've got a few last calculations to do, but they
        can wait.

                    RIVERS
        You brought champagne?

Alex smiles, as if wishing he'd thought of the idea himself.

                    ALEX
        Come morning, we're going to witness the ultimate
        cosmic catastrophe. If that doesn't call for a bit of the
        bubbly, I don't know what does.

WILLOW
(forced cheeriness)
I'll drink to that. I'll even pour–
(hesitates)
–if it's OK with everybody.

Kristen hesitates, then hands Willow the bottle with a slight smile. Willow smiles back. Everyone but Swayzey seems in a good mood. The expedition's become a real group, at last.

DISSOLVE TO:

EXT. THE SKY - NIGHT
The Comet and its tail already seem to loom a bit larger.

HAUPT (O.S.)
I'm glad it's a comet instead of a meteor. The end
of a world should be a thing of terrifying beauty.

EXT. THE CAMPSITE - NIGHT
The group sit around a fire–Willow makes the rounds, pouring champagne into plastic cups. Open tins and plates show they've eaten. Kristen sits with Rivers–Cyrano atop a shrub. Featherstone keeps far from Haupt. A rudimentary thorny-shrub boma now surrounds the camp for protection.

From where he's cuffed nearby, Swayzey glowers at them. An uneaten plate of food sits near him, but no cup of champagne.

HAUPT (cont'd)
But let's face it–none of us would be celebrating if it
was the human race that was about to be wiped off
the face of the Earth, instead of the dinosaurs and half
the other species currently on the planet.
(as Willow sits, the open bottle by her)
Still, I propose a toast–to the end of one world, and
the beginning of another!

130

All "clink" cups and sip–except Featherstone. Willow sets her cup down, barely touched.

> KRISTEN
> Will the Comet's impact really wipe out species all over the world?

Firelight on his face, Haupt is a soft-spoken prophet of doom, as the others sip the rest of their champagne.

> HAUPT
> The earthquakes, the tidal wave, the forest fires will be strictly a western-hemisphere phenomenon. But when all the dust kicked up by the impact is spread throughout the upper atmosphere, it'll become so dark all over the world that you couldn't see your hand in front of your face.

> BO
> Just like in the Bible, huh?
>> (as the others look)
> "And there was a thick darkness in all the land of Egypt three days. They saw not one another, neither rose any from his place..."
>> (smiles at the group)
> Preacher's son. Comes with the territory.

The others smile, a bit uncomfortably. Kristen snuggles into the crook of Rivers' arm. He's surprised but stays put as she leans against him as if for protection. Haupt goes on:

> HAUPT
> The darkness, and the cold that goes with it, will last for months. When that ends, there'll be nitric acid rain, followed by a greenhouse effect that'll make the global warming we worry about look like a brisk fall day.

131

KRISTEN
What could live through all that?

Haupt looks off, envisioning another world. As he speaks, Willow glances at Swayzey, sullenly facing away from them. She picks up her cupful of champagne and walks around to him. Kristen notices, nudges Rivers–he indicates it's OK.

HAUPT
The dinosaurs will be totally wiped out, of course.
Many plant species will die during the cold and dark–
that means the big herbivores will starve, and so will
the carnosaurs that feed on them. Also lots of sea life.
Birds, which have only been around since the Jurassic, will come close to going extinct, as well.

Willow offers the champagne to Swayzey. He glares at her–then knocks the glass out of her hand. She looks at him a moment, then walks off. Kristen fills the awkward silence:

KRISTEN
Yet many birds must have survived–and smaller
reptiles and mammals–

HAUPT
Enough of them, anyway. After first the cold and
then the heat go away, they'll thrive–and slowly begin to create the world we know.

WILLOW
This must be what God feels like.

Everyone looks at her–she stands outside their circle.

WILLOW (cont'd)
I mean–just like God, we know what's going to
happen, don't we–for the next 65 million years?

HAUPT
The big picture, yes–but a lot of the details are fuzzy.
And like they say, "The devil is in the details."

Willow looks at him, puzzled. So does Kristen.

RIVERS
What he means is, we know the dinosaurs are
doomed, starting tomorrow–just as we know that,
millions of years later, Adolf Hitler will kill six
million Jews. But that doesn't mean there's anything
we can do about either event.

The group shift, uncomfortable. Willow approaches the circle,

WILLOW
Why can't you stop him?

RIVERS
Who?

WILLOW
Hitler. Why don't you just go back to before World
War Two and shoot the rat bastard?

ALEX
(jumps in)
Prochaska claims there's a time-travel Law of
Unintended Consequences. If you shoot Hitler,
there's always a risk that interfering with history
might cause something even even worse.
(at Willow's look)
Hard to imagine, I know, but we can't be 100%
certain it couldn't happen.

RIVERS

Though I'm sure there's plenty of people who'd risk
it–and shoot the rat bastard.

He smiles at Willow. Kristen sits up, leaving the crook of his
arm. Mild regret shows on his otherwise impassive face.

KRISTEN
(to Rivers and Alex)
How far back do you have to go before there's no
chance you'll just–step on a butterfly or something–
and change things so the Nazis win the war? Or
Carthage levels Rome?

ALEX
Or Ben Franklin gets struck by lightning flying his
kite?
(Kristen nods)
The Professor calculates at least 100,000 B.C., give
or take a few millennia. Before then, anything we do
is lost in the stream of time before human history begins.
(beat)
Even so, once we've visited a stretch of time, it isn't
safe to return to it–since the Cube and anybody in it
can't exist twice in the same time. That Time Para-
dox thing he talked about at the press conference.

Kristen nods to say she understands. Rivers and Alex rise.

RIVERS
That's it. Everybody get some sleep. Even you,
Dr. Haupt, if you can. We need everybody sharp in
the morning.

ALEX

We don't want to be stumbling over each other when
the Comet hits.

Bruce distributes a stash of sleeping-bags as the group file by.
As Kristen shifts her Ultra-Cam so she can take one:

KRISTEN

I won't be using the shots of Holtzinger being killed,
but I could use some more footage before we leave.

ALEX

At dawn we'll take you downslope. An hour should
give McMurtrie his money's worth. It's to our
benefit, too.

RIVERS
(indicates Alex's arm)
I'll take her. Bo stays with you. We need at least one
man in camp who can handle the .1000 in case our
Giganoto comes back.

SWAYZEY
(a sneer in his voice)
I can handle one.

ALEX
(to Rivers)
I hope you think an invalid like me is up to taking
first watch.

RIVERS
(smiles)
Wake me in three hours.

Alex stomps off, with his .600, out of camp and downslope.

EXT. CAMPSITE

Minutes later. Rivers, preparing his sleeping-bag at one end of camp, pauses, stares off into the woods. Kristen comes up.

                    KRISTEN
          Still thinking about Holtzinger?
                    (no response)
          There was nothing you could have done. And it's a
          year ago now...

                    RIVERS
          In this world, it's a year. To that thing that killed him,
          it's a year.
                    (touches his temple)
          But not in here.

                    KRISTEN
          Poor Rivers...

Rivers puts his hands on her shoulders, starts to draw her to him. She disengages gently.

                    KRISTEN (cont'd)
          We'll probably both get more sleep if I bed down
          at the far end of camp.

                    RIVERS
                    (drops his hands)
          Sure. Whatever.

She moves off, her sleeping-bag under her arm. Rivers watches her go, and shakes his head. Women... He YAWNS.

The others, some also YAWNING, place their sleeping-bags fairly close to each other, as if there's safety in numbers. Willow beds down a bit apart, near Cyrano's shrub.

The fire burns on, hopefully keeping any predators at bay.

DISSOLVE TO:

EXT. EDGE OF CAMP - NIGHT
Slightly downslope from camp, but still outside the circling forest, Alex stands at his post near a large, lone tree.

Abruptly, there's the CRACK of a twig somewhere off in among the trees. Alex, alert, hefts his .600.

Something watches Alex from yards away, through the trees–something circling slowly around him.

Alex hears no more and relaxes slightly. He looks up at the Comet. As he does so, he YAWNS–which surprises him. He slaps his face a couple of times and renews his effort to keep an alert eye on the downslope forest.

DISSOLVE TO:

EXT. CAMPSITE - NIGHT
Swayzey, dozing. A CLICK. Swayzey starts, surprised–then sees his handcuffs have been unlocked. He looks around.

So far as he can see, everyone is asleep near the fire, beneath a Comet grown even larger overhead. Even Haupt has dozed off, sitting at his spectro-telescope.

Swayzey eases out of the cuffs and crawls toward Bo, who SNORES nearby, hand on his .600. As Swayzey touches the rifle, Bo SNORTS, as if about to wake. Swayzey recoils.

He creeps off silently–but not yet out of camp.

DISSOLVE TO:

EXT. THE DOWNSLOPE FOREST - NIGHT
A MONTAGE of half-natural-speed images reliving the pre-
vious year's tragedy–a continual ROARING the only SOUND
we hear:

Rivers racing up the slope through the shrubs–

Swayzey trying to reload as Alex drags Holtzinger his way–

The Giganotosaurus roaring as it charges the trio–

Swayzey dropping his shells and kneeling–Alex and Holtzinger falling, Alex striking his head and arm–

Rivers running, running–but he's moving in SUPER-SLOW
MOTION–everything else moves at mere half-speed–

The Giganotosaurus looming, roaring, above the trio–

Holtzinger grabbing his .500 and firing up, missing–

Rivers running full out - but even slower now, as if through
invisible molasses–stopping, still far from the Giganotosaurus
–firing at the beast as it turns its head–

The bullet digging a bloody trench in the Giganotosaurus'
cheek–

Holtzinger aiming his rifle up at the beast again–

The Giganotosaurus glaring down at Holtzinger–

Rivers runs closer in SLOMO–stops to aim his rifle–

The Giganotosaurus dipping its head to engulf the top half of
Holtzinger–then rearing up, his feet still twitching–

Rivers can't fire–might hit Holtzinger–

The Giganotosaurus stalking off with Holtzinger's legs, barely seen from the back, still sticking out of its mouth–

Rivers stares in horror–CAMERA ZOOMS IN to a CLOSE-UP–

EXT. CLOSE ON RIVERS - NIGHT (PRE-DAWN)
He wakes up, sweating. CAMERA PULLS BACK, to reveal–

EXT. CAMPSITE - NIGHT (PRE-DAWN)
Below, the sleeping camp–overhead, the Comet, now larger than ever and nearer the southeastern horizon, has made the night even brighter. Rivers has been having a nightmare.

The fire abruptly CRACKLES as a burning log shifts and drops.

Rivers starts at the sound, then gazes around at his sleeping comrades. After a moment, he holds his head–it hurts.

His eyes fall on the shrub to which Swayzey was bound–the handcuffs are empty, and Swayzey is gone.

Rivers leaps to his feet, his .1000 in hand. He sees Haupt asleep where he sits–sees Bo SNORING, hand on his .600–Bruce's rifle lying near him–Featherstone tossing in sleep.

Kristen's bag, the farthest off, is crumpled as if her back is turned to us–Rivers doesn't go any nearer.

River sees that Willow's sleeping-bag, near Cyrano, is empty.

He moves stealthily toward the periphery of the camp, trying not to awaken anyone–not that that's hard.

EXT. EDGE OF CAMP - NIGHT (PRE-DAWN)

Rivers sees Alex from behind, downslope, leaning against the lone tree. He taps Alex–the big Sioux wakes with a start.

> ALEX
>
> What–?

Alex tries to focus on Rivers–he's having trouble getting fully awake. He puts his hands to his pounding head.

> ALEX
>
> I was asleep? My God–I never in my life–

> RIVERS
>
> It was the champagne. Swayzey and Willow are gone. Guess she decided he was her best bet, after all.
> (looks up at the Comet)
> It's almost dawn.

Alex wakes fully at last–the full import of Rivers' words sinks in on him. River strides back toward camp. As Alex falls in beside him, he feels in his pocket for the cuff keys.

> ALEX
>
> She must've lifted the keys. The guns–?

> RIVERS
>
> All .600s accounted for. They must've had to run off unarmed.

EXT. THE CAMPSITE - NIGHT (PRE-DAWN) (CONTINUOUS)

Rivers and Alex reach the camp. Alex SHOUTS:

> ALEX
>
> Everybody up!

At his apparatus, Haupt sits up abruptly. Bo, Bruce and Featherstone also wake. All have difficulty getting alert.

Rivers notices Kristen hasn't stirred. He moves to her sleeping-bag, which is shaped as if her back is turned to him.

> RIVERS
>> Kristen...?

No response. He nudges the bag with his foot–his boot sinks into it. Crouching, he turns the sleeping-bag over and is shocked to see it's empty. Kristen is gone–so is her Ultra-Cam. Alex sees this as he strides up with Bo and Bruce:

> BO
>> Swayzey must've wanted a hostage.

Rivers says nothing, his face a mask. He looks down at several empty cups and the empty champagne bottle, lying nearby.

> ALEX
>> I'm coming with you.

> RIVERS
>> (shakes his head)
>> Out there in the bush, you'd just slow me down.
>> You three get everybody ready to go.

Alex, Bo and Bruce glance up at the Comet. For a moment they'd forgotten it. Haupt and Featherstone shamble over, still dazed. Rivers hands Bo the .1000, checks out his .600.

> RIVERS (cont'd)
>> (to all)
>> The .600'll do me. The plan stays the same: Soon as
>> you see the flash of the impact, you know you've
>> only got–

HAUPT
(talking over him)
Twenty-one minutes.

RIVERS
–21 minutes till the shock wave hits. I want you out
of here with at least a minute to spare–even that's
cutting it close. If I'm not back, you leave without
me.

ALEX
No! He isn't worth it!

RIVERS
The hell with Swayzey. I've got to see if I can
save her.

Haupt and Featherstone exchange a glance, confused.

BO
Swayzey and his squeeze took Kristen.

Rivers' face betrays nothing of what he may be thinking, as he
fastens a switched-off flat flashlight to his belt.

HAUPT
Just so we don't have to leave before we see the impact. It's the only way we can ever be sure–

RIVERS
You'll have your front-row seat to doomsday. But if
you stick around too long, you'll be part of the show.

HAUPT
(looks around)
Kristen's camera–maybe we can film–

ALEX

Swayzey took it, too—God knows why.

RIVERS

Remember, Bruce, 20 minutes after impact, no more—
then—

BRUCE
(swallows hard)
Back to the future.

RIVERS
(grins)
You got it.

He turns and strides out of camp, rifle in hand. The others
watch him go until his figure is lost among the trees below—

Bo, Alex and Featherstone begin loading equipment into the
Chrono-Cube. Haupt feverishly works his computer/spectro-
telescope, striving to record all the data he can.

DISSOLVE TO:

EXT. THE FOREST DOWNSLOPE - NIGHT (PRE-DAWN)
Rivers moves silently, swiftly. Though it's dark where trees
hide the Comet's light, he leaves the flash on his 'belt.

He stops—spotting a small piece from Willow's blouse on a
jutting branch off to one side. He veers in that direction.

Rivers' foot comes down on the tip of a scaly tail.

Rivers recoils as a dark shape looms. He grasps his flashlight
and turns it on, ready to fire—

In its beam is a STEGOCERAS (not a Stegosaur)—a ridge-headed plant-eater only 6-7 feet long, and only 4-5 feet tall as it rears up, frightened. It BLEETS goat-like and runs off.

Rivers breathes easier, turns off the flashlight and runs on.

EXT. LEVEL FOREST - NIGHT (PRE-DAWN)
Rivers pauses on a natural trail made by dinosaurs—he listens. He hears a SOUND ahead—so he veers off the trail into the woods—stalking silently as a panther.

Rivers peers through trees as he nears a clearing—

EXT. SMALL CLEARING - NIGHT (PRE-DAWN)
Swayzey and Willow have stopped here. He PANTS—she sprawls breathless. Above a low line of trees on the southeast horizon, the Comet is brightly visible.

> WILLOW
> Des—for God's sake—

> SWAYZEY
> This is as far as you go.

With effort, Swayzey snaps a big limb off a tree and turns menacingly toward Willow. Her eyes are wide with fear.

> SWAYZEY
> I'd have strangled you back in camp, but I couldn't risk waking the others.

Rivers tries to aim his .600, but trees obscure his view as Swayzey moves around, brandishing the limb. Suddenly, Rivers hears the SNAP of a twig off to one side—freezes—then, hearing nothing more, he turns back toward Swayzey and Willow.

Swayzey stalks toward Willow. Scooting away, she finds herself up against a fallen trunk. Swayzey raises the limb–

                    WILLOW
        Please, Des–

                    SWAYZEY
        You dumb little bitch–setting me free–

                    WILLOW
        But I didn't!

Willow's protest makes Swayzey pause for a crucial moment–
Rivers plows into him, and the two go down, rolling.

Swayzey rolls free and swings the thick limb at Rivers' skull–
Rivers raises the .600 between his hands, blocking the blow–
then kicks up, knocking Swayzey back–

But the limb's smaller branches catch on the .600 and pull it
out of Rivers' hands. As it falls, it goes off–BLAM!

EXT. THE FOREST - AERIAL VIEW - NIGHT (PRE-DAWN)
The shot REVERBERATES beneath the sky in which the
Comet looms large, not far above the southeastern horizon.

                                        CUT TO:

EXT. ANOTHER PART OF THE FOREST - NIGHT (PRE-DAWN)
A beat, as the shot SOUND FADES. An enormous head rises,
filling the screen–the Giganotosaurus, identifiable by wide
scar tissue on one cheek. It moves off SNARLING toward the
SOUND–as dawn begins to lighten the horizon.

                                        CUT TO:

EXT. CAMPSITE - NIGHT (PRE-DAWN)

Alex, Bo and Featherstone stop loading the Chrono-Cube as the shot ECHOES. Haupt looks up from his computer screen. Bo grabs his gun and starts toward the trees. Alex lays a hand on his arm and shakes his head. All go back to work.

CAMERA MOVES UP to the sky—where the Comet, quite large now, fills much of the southeastern horizon as dawn nears—

DISSOLVE TO:

EXT. SMALL CLEARING - NIGHT (PRE-DAWN)

CAMERA MOVES DOWN from sky, which gradually lightens during what follows—to reveal Rivers squared off with Swayzey, each seeking an opening—Willow watches in horror.

Swayzey picks up another jagged branch and swings it at Rivers. Rivers dodges one swing, then another.

Swayzey swings the branch again, at the same time making a crouching grab for the fallen .600.

Rivers takes the blow, which cuts his side. Despite the pain, Rivers grabs hold of the branch and pulls.

Swayzey is pulled forward, but manages to grab hold of the rifle barrel—he swings the weapon awkwardly at Rivers.

The rifle butt strikes Rivers' forehead.

Rivers falls sprawling, his temple bleeding. Swayzey fumbles with the rifle, trying to bring it into position to shoot him.

Willow lunges forward, grabbing the barrel. Swayzey slugs her in the face. Bleeding from the nose, she's knocked into Rivers as he's rising–both tumble to the ground.

Smirking, Swayzey aims the .600 at Rivers, who's shielded only by Willow lying awkwardly across him.

> SWAYZEY
> I'll bet one bullet'll go through both of you.

> KRISTEN (O.S.)
> Actually, that would make a nice composition.

All three turn in surprise–

Kristen moves toward them slowly out of the forest. She holds her camcorder at eye-level, apparently filming.

> KRISTEN
> Smile, Mr. Swayzey. You're on "The Primeval's Funniest Home Videos."

Swayzey sneers at Kristen–keeps the .600 on Rivers, who's getting to his feet. Rivers is horrified to see Kristen.

Kristen takes a step toward Swayzey. He aims the gun at her.

> KRISTEN
> Am I really supposed to believe you'd waste your last shell and let Rivers get you?

> SWAYZEY
> Take another step and I'll smash your face in.

Kristen takes that step, still aiming her camera at Swayzey.

SWAYZEY
I warned you, bitch–

He stalks toward Kristen, the limb upraised.

FWIT! The SOUND of compressed air–Swayzey stops short, a startled look on his face. We can't see what happened–

Then he spins around, mouth open–a round crimson hole between his eyes. Blood only now begins to trickle out–and Swayzey falls dead at Willow's feet, gun still in hand.

WILLOW
She shot him? With a camera?

Willow, confused, looks from Rivers to Kristen and back again. Rivers starts toward Kristen–she swings her camera around so it points at him.

RIVERS
You going to use that silencer on me, too?

WILLOW
Silencer? What the hell's going on?

Kristen keeps the Ultra-Cam pointed at Rivers, ignoring her.

KRISTEN
When did you know?

RIVERS
When I really thought about the champagne. If Willow'd spiked it, she wouldn't have offered Swayzey any if she was planning to help him escape–

WILLOW
(over his words)
I didn't spike a damn thing! What're you talking
about?

RIVERS
(without pausing)
—so it had to be drugged from the start. And that
meant you.
(beat)
Originally, you planned to get to Swayzey through
me, but then you realized you'd have a better chance
through McMurtrie.

KRISTEN
You didn't take women on safari—but a man with
McMurtrie's ego, not to mention sex drive—
(Rivers reacts)
—it wasn't hard to get to him, then arrange that hit-
and-run so I could replace him.

THE FOREST
Something moves amid the trees—it circles the small clearing,
watching as Rivers and Willow face Kristen.

RIVERS
Not that you've actually filmed anything since we
got here.

KRISTEN
(indicates camera)
There's room in here for a gun or camera works, not
both. I could have shot Swayzey at the zoo, or the
moment he walked into Prochaska's lab—

RIVERS
But his goons were always around. Only he didn't
think he needed them where the only threat was wild
animals.

THE SMALL CLEARING
Rivers circles, seeking an opening—at the same time he keeps
one eye on the Comet, which has moved perceptibly lower
toward the southeastern dawn-horizon. Kristen keeps the camera aimed at him and ignores Willow, who stands rooted.

RIVERS (cont'd)
Back here there'd likely be a chance for you to kill
him and let us think a dinosaur got him.

WILLOW
You mean she's—?

RIVERS
Part of a rival mob—or else their paid assassin.

KRISTEN
Right the second time. I freed Swayzey while the rest
of you slept off a Mickey. A very light one—I needed
you awake before the Comet hit.

Rivers stops opposite Kristen—Willow off to one side. He
glances toward the horizon.

The Comet is very low now—almost at the horizon line of distant trees, to the south of the coming sunrise.

KRISTEN (cont'd)
If he'd gone for a gun, I'd have shot him in camp and
taken my chances. But he ran, and dragging this
bimbo along slowed him down.

WILLOW

Hey–

She takes a step toward Kristen. Kristen pivots the camera
around at her–Willow stops cold.

KRISTEN

I'm not limited to two shots like your boy friend was.

WILLOW

So why haven't you shot us already, instead of trying
to talk us to death?

KRISTEN
(to Rivers)

I wanted you to know before you died. Call it
professional courtesy. One great hunter to another.

RIVERS

You're a hired killer, nothing more. The greatest
event anyone'll ever witness is practically on top of
us, and you're filling a murder contract.

KRISTEN

When half the life on Earth is about to be wiped out,
what do three more lives matter?
(sights camera)
You first, Rivers...

She's starting to squeeze the "trigger" when she sees Rivers
glance toward the horizon–she follows his gaze–

The coming sunrise is already fairly bright. The Comet just
above the southeast horizon seems unmoving–then it begins
visibly to move–very slightly, yet picking up a little speed
with each second–moving down toward the horizon.

                            RIVERS
              Comet's hitting the atmosphere...

Rivers, Willow and Kristen stare frozen at this phenomenon.

The Comet, gaining speed, continues to descend–till, with a
last quickening, it disappears below the horizon. A beat.

                         RIVERS (O.S.)
              Gravity's taken hold...

All three watch, mesmerized. Rivers WHISPERS to Willow:

                            RIVERS
              Close your eyes–tight.

She does.

On the horizon, a GLOW appears. Between it and the sunrise,
It's as if two suns were rising at the same time, a right angle
apart–but the new "sunrise" brightens must faster–

                         RIVERS (O.S.)
              It's hit.

Suddenly, there's a blaze of light, many times brighter than
the Sun–filling the screen, blotting out even the sunrise.

All three are washed by the brilliance–Rivers' and Willow's
eyes are closed–Kristen, caught with eyes open, is briefly
blinded.

On the southeast horizon, the brilliance fades–a crimson, illu-
minated dome rises there, expands both upward and outward,

The clearing is washed by crimson light. Rivers grabs Willow and pulls her toward the trees. FWIT! Kristen, still half-blind, misses Rivers.

Kristen FWITS another burst after them as they reach the trees. Stepping over the .600, she stalks after them.

EXT. THE FOREST PRIMEVAL - AERIAL VIEW - DAY (DAWN)
The crimson dome continues to spread, though slowing–its color has darkened and faded slightly.

EXT. ANOTHER PART OF THE FOREST - DAY (DAWN)
Rivers moves fast as he can, dragging Willow. She stumbles, GROANS–he pulls her roughly to her feet.

> WILLOW
> That crudhead–
> (off Rivers' look)
> He thought I set him free–and he still tried to kill me!

Rivers drags her off into the trees.

> DISSOLVE TO:

EXT. THE FOREST - DAY
Willow does her best to keep up with Rivers–branches tear savagely at their clothes.

> WILLOW
> Shouldn't we be back at camp by now?

> RIVERS
> We had to circle around.

> WILLOW
> How long have we got?

                         RIVERS
              Twenty minutes–from when the Comet hit.

Willow's eyes widen. He alters direction, dragging her along.

                                                    CUT TO:

EXT. THE FOREST - DAY
Kristen moves quickly through trees and underbrush–she's
cold, determined and far more at home in the outdoors than
she'd pretended. Smallish dinosaurs race out of her path.

                                                    CUT TO:

EXT. THE FOREST - DAY
Beneath the sky glow, the Giganotosaurus stalks the woods–it
stops to SNIFF the breeze, then moves on.

                                                    CUT TO:

EXT. THE FOREST - DAY (DAWN)
Rivers and Willow have doubled back–Rivers pauses. Willow
collapses onto a log, PANTING–she looks at him curiously.

                         WILLOW
           What?

                         RIVERS
              Thought I heard something.

                         WILLOW
              We're surrounded by hot-and-cold running dinosaurs,
              and we're being stalked by an armed killer. Now, I'm
              just taking a wild stab here–but you think maybe it
              could be one of them?

                           154

                    RIVERS
        No. This was–something else.

                    WILLOW
        Why don't I like the way you said that?

                    RIVERS
        Come on... you're doing great.

He pulls her up, gently as he can under the circumstances–and
they're off again...

                                    DISSOLVE TO:

<u>EXT. CAMPSITE - DAY</u>
The Chrono-Cube sits loaded–Cyrano perched atop the spectro-telescope. Alex and Bo peer anxiously downslope. On
board, Featherstone and Haupt nervously watch the sky. Bruce
stops adjusting controls, looks at his watch.

                    BRUCE
        We've gotta go.

                    ALEX
        Just give him another few minutes.

Bo and Bruce exchange a look. This is dangerous. But Alex
keeps peering off downslope...

                                    CUT TO:

<u>EXT. THE FOREST - DAY</u>
Rivers and Willow moving along–the ground slopes slightly
upward now–they reach a juncture where several long-fallen
trees, piled in a jumble like jackstraws, block their way.

                         RIVERS
Shit.

                         WILLOW
That's just what I was gonna say.

He scrambles agilely up the pile of trees and peers beyond.

                         RIVERS
Once we're over this, we're just ten minutes
from camp.

                         WILLOW
How much time we got left?

                         RIVERS
                    (glances at watch)
You don't want to know.

He reaches down his hand. Willow stretches out to grasp it
and starts to climb. But she's barely begun when–

                    KRISTEN (O.S.)
Hold that pose!

Kristen, winded but no less determined, moves out into the
clear area near the jumble of trees, her gun/camera in hand.
She smiles.

                         RIVERS
You've got no beef with Willow. Let her go.

                         KRISTEN
I'm a professional, Rivers. No loose ends.
                    (aims the gun/camera)
Say cheese. . .

                           156

Rivers and Willow brace for the bullets.

Kristen is about to press the trigger–when the sharp, bloody point of a crude spear juts out of her chest. With a look of puzzlement, she drops the gun/camera and falls on her face– dead. The spear's handle juts out her back.

Rivers and Willow exchange a questioning glance, where Willow virtually dangles from his outstretched hand.

Next moment, there's a SAVAGE, INCOHERENT YELL–

A WILD MAN bursts into the open–he seems almost an ani- mal, with long stringy hair, dirt-smudged face and limbs, his scant clothing a makeshift mix of tattered safari garb and small-mammal skins woven together.

His YELL ECHOES as he moves with blurring speed to Kristen's corpse, places his foot on her back and pulls out his spear.

Willow slips from Rivers' grasp–with a SHRIEK she falls near the Wild Man–he raises his bloody spear above the sprawled Willow, poised to thrust it down into her–

RIVERS

No–!

The Wild Man pauses, gazes up at the astonished Rivers. He's almost unrecognizable as he SNARLS up through jagged teeth, and yet–

RIVERS (O.S.)

Holtzinger–?

CUT TO:

EXT. CAMPSITE - DAY (DAWN)

The three in the Chrono-Cube are really antsy now. Bruce calls to Bo, who stands next to the slope-scanning Alex:

> BRUCE
> Alex–in God's name–

> ALEX
> Just one more minute!

Bo puts his hand on Alex's shoulder–shakes his head.

> BO
> Rivers wouldn't want us to still be here.

A beat. Alex nods reluctantly and moves with Bo toward the Cube, still dragging his feet. Bruce is near-frantic.

> BRUCE
> Hurry up, you guys!

> CUT TO:

EXT. THE SLOPE - CLEAR AREA - DAY

As Rivers stares down into the Wild Man/Holtzinger's eyes, Holtzinger SNARLS above the terrified Willow.

> HOLTZINGER
> Rivers. . .

His voice is that of a man who's had no one to talk to in so long that he's almost forgotten how to speak. His specs are long gone.

> WILLOW
> That's Holtzinger? August Holtzinger? He sure
> looks different from this morning...

RIVERS
To him that was a year ago. When I think of what he
must've gone through in that year–

HOLTZINGER
(to Rivers; hostile)
You–did this to me.

Rivers sees Willow creeping away, so he stalls:

RIVERS
How'd you manage to survive? We saw
that Giganoto carry you off.

Holtzinger seems to be seeing events a million years away.

HOLTZINGER
I was–in its mouth–my gun went off again–must've
hurt it–it dropped me–

Holtzinger shoves aside fur and cloth, revealing his middle–a
mass of scar tissue.

HOLTZINGER (cont'd)
Hurt–I was hurt bad. But I got better–got strong–
had to get strong–or die–

As he remembers, he clenches his fists–his arm–and shoulder-
muscles are hardened cords. This Wild Man could strangle the
Holtzinger of a year ago without breathing hard.

HOLTZINGER (cont'd)
I was hiding–hiding, all the time–ate what the meat-
eaters left–learned to set traps–make spears–always
hungry–always–

Rivers sees what surviving for a year in the primeval has done for–and to–Holtzinger, and it pains him.

> HOLTZINGER (cont'd)
> Been here a long time–
> > (mulling it over)
> –long time.

> RIVERS
> > (passionately)
> We can help you, Holtzinger. We'll take you back home–back to your wife.

Holtzinger looks wistful, as if trying hard to remember her.

> CUT TO:

EXT. THE CLEARING - THE CHRONO-CUBE - DAY
Alex, Bo, Haupt and Featherstone are all in the Chrono-Cube–
Alex and Bo peer anxiously toward the woods, hoping Rivers will appear–Bruce frantically works the controls.

> FEATHERSTONE
> What's wrong?

> BRUCE
> It starts up slow sometime. But don't worry, it'll–
> > (as HUM begins)
> That's got it. It'll take just a few seconds...

> BO
> Good, 'cause that's about what we got!

Grim, tense, they wait–there's nothing else they can do.

> CUT TO:

EXT. CLEAR AREA BY JUMBLE OF TREES - DAY

Rivers looks down at Holtzinger. Willow has stumbled to her feet, a few yards off.

                    RIVERS
          Put down the spear, Holtzinger–we can take
          you back.

SNARLING, Holtzinger suddenly rears back, grasping his spear.

                    HOLTZINGER
          No! Too late–for that.
                    (glares with hatred)
          You let that thing get me–left me here! I belong here
          now–but you belong–dead!

He gets set to hurl his spear up at Rivers.

Rivers leaps from atop the jumble of trees–he smashes into Holtzinger before he can throw his spear. The men crash to the rough ground, as Willow SCREAMS.

Rivers and Holtzinger struggle–Rivers lands a solid punch–it fazes Holtzinger, but he grabs Rivers–

With a strength honed by his year in hell, Holtzinger picks the astonished Rivers up bodily and hurls him several yards–he falls hard.

Next moment, Holtzinger is on top of Rivers–his powerful fingers about Rivers' neck–squeezing–

Willow leaps onto Holtzinger's back–her fingernails rake his face–

Holtzinger elbows her off with a strong blow to the solar plexus–she falls breathless to the ground.

But her action gave Rivers a chance to work one arm free–he belts Holtzinger, knocking him backward into the jumble of trees–Holtzinger's clothes get snagged on a branch–

Rivers scrambles to one knee–

> RIVERS
> Snap out of it, Holtzinger! We haven't got time for this.

A RUMBLE has started low but swiftly gets louder, louder, till it nearly drowns out his words–he shouts at Willow:

> RIVERS
> The shock wave!

Holtzinger is too far gone to hear the SOUND, or feel the slight trembling of earth that has begun. Tearing free of the branches, he grabs his spear and is about to hurl it.

Suddenly, amid a DEAFENING RUMBLE, Rivers, Holtzinger and Willow are thrown to the ground. All they can do is be bounced around as the shock wave (transmitted by both air and ground) washes over them–on its way up the slope.

CUT TO:

EXT. CAMPSITE - DAY (DAWN)
The five men in the Chrono-Cube are tense as the HUM rises. But now, starting under the HUM but swiftly rising to drown it out is a sinister growing RUMBLE–they react with alarm as the Cube begins to quiver, then to shake violently–

They look downslope toward the southeastern horizon and see the ground and trees there trembling–in a wavelike line fast moving toward them–and they know what it is.

Bruce desperately works the controls–the SHIMMER OF LIGHT slowly begins to pulse around the Cube–

But it's too late! The undulating wave of air and earth reaches the Cube and smites it like a living thing–

The Cube bounces so hard it topples over on its side–the men and equipment inside are sent tumbling–

Heavy apparatus, including a tarpaulin, falls toward Cyrano– Bo makes a grab at him–Cyrano flies off, downslope toward the forest.

Bo's lunge puts him in the way of the falling apparatus–it pins him painfully under it, as the others half-scramble, half-fall out of the Cube. Bo's .1000 goes flying.

A crevice several yards wide opens shudderingly between the fallen Cube and the direction downslope taken by Rivers. The .1000 winds up on the far side of the crevice.

Earth and air continue to undulate and tremble–no one can get to his feet, let alone try to help Bo.

CUT TO:

EXT. THE CLEAR AREA - DAY (DAWN)
As the Earth trembles, Rivers reaches Willow–she clings to him–Holtzinger is bounced around–the jumbled trees are tossed about like tenpins, partly clearing the path upslope.

With a great CRACK, a yawning crevice opens under Holtzinger.

His YELL drowned out, Holtzinger topples in–one out-stretched hand barely manages to grasp the lip of the crevice–several of the jackstrawed trees also fall in.

Then the shock wave has passed. Earth's trembling subsides. Rivers helps Willow to her feet, and helps her scramble over the only tree trunk remaining in their path upslope–

                    HOLTZINGER
          Rivers–!

Rivers turns back to see Holtzinger clinging to the lip of the crevice. He lets go of Willow and races back to him.

                    WILLOW
          Are you crazy?

Rivers grabs Holtzinger's hand and looks into his wild eyes. He pulls hard, but it's not quite enough. Rivers looks back at Willow. She hesitates–then runs to him, throws her arms around his waist, and pulls.

                    WILLOW
          OK, so we're both crazy!

Together they haul Holtzinger up–all three sprawl on the crevice lip, breathing hard. Rivers starts to rise:

                    RIVERS
          Come on. The Cube's probably long gone by
          now, but–

Holtzinger SNARLS like the madman he has become and grabs Willow. He lifts her over his head and holds her above the crevice. She SHRIEKS. Rivers lunges toward him–

                              RIVERS
          Holtzinger–no!

Holtzinger hurls Willow SCREAMING into the crevice. Rivers throws himself down on the lip and stares into the abyss.

Willow has landed hard on one of the tree trunks that had toppled in–it's jammed precariously between opposite sides of the crevice–she's holding on to the trunk, her legs dangling in space. She looks up at him, desperate.

Rivers glances at Holtzinger, who's crouching to leap–then back to Willow. Ignoring his own peril, Rivers reaches one arm down toward her–

She strains to reach his outstretched fingers, only inches away–now less than an inch, and yet–

The tree shifts with a GROAN under Willow, and drops away–just as Rivers' and Willow's fingers interlock.

Willow dangles maddeningly over the yawning abyss, held only by the interlocking of her and Rivers' fingers.

As Rivers strains beneath Willow's weight, he looks up at Holtzinger–a plea for mercy for Willow in his eyes.

But there's no mercy in the crouching Holtzinger's wild gaze. Rivers braces himself–Holtzinger springs toward him.

Suddenly, a huge head swoops down INTO FRAME–and engulfs Holtzinger in mid-leap!

Rivers looks up, his eyes wide–

The scar-cheeked Giganotosaurus has Holtzinger's upper half engulfed, much as before–blood runs down Holtzinger's legs where saber-length fangs have pierced him.

The Giganotosaurus CHOMPS, shakes–the lower half of Holtzinger's body drops away–and falls past Rivers, into the crevice–

FOREST AND CREVICE
Holtzinger's severed pelvis and legs topple past the dangling, swaying, SCREAMING Willow.

As the Giganotosaurus gulps down the half of Holtzinger he has bitten off, Rivers desperately pulls at Willow.

Willow manages to brace her legs against the side of the crevice–

Rivers hauls her up–Willow gawks, paralyzed with fear, at the towering Giganotosaurus, CHOMPING on its meal. Rivers picks her up and races up the slope in the direction of the camp.

The Giganotosaurus GULPS down the last of Holtzinger's trunk–then peers down into the crevice where the rest of him vanished. Seeing nothing, it stalks off upslope after the humans who just fled.

EXT. FORESTED SLOPE - DAY
Rivers carries Willow along–she looks past his shoulder–the Giganotosaurus is gaining on them, no doubt about it.

> WILLOW
> You think he remembers you're the one shot him?

> RIVERS
> I'm starting to think so.

Willow, aware of a red glow on her face, looks skyward. It's as if dozens, hundreds of shooting stars, fiery enough to be seen in daytime, are suddenly raining out of the sky.

One of the "shooting stars" strikes the ground right in front of Rivers–he and Willow are hurled to the ground.

The "shooting stars" are striking all around them now–setting fire even to the greenest of trees with their incandescent heat, as Rivers SHOUTS:

> RIVERS
>
> The ejecta!

> WILLOW
>
> The who?

> RIVERS
>
> Fragments of the Comet, and everything else spewed up by the impact–they're finally coming back down.

They scramble to their feet as more fiery ejecta fall. They look behind them:

The Giganotosaurus has stopped, puzzled–it ROARS a mixture of defiance and fear at the heavens.

Seen past the Giganotosaurus, the ejecta are causing more and more fires amid the trees. They haven't all joined yet, but–

> RIVERS
>
> We're in for one helluva forest fire.

He pulls Willow upslope as ejecta strike around them.

CUT TO:

<u>EXT. CAMPSITE - DAY</u>
Beneath a sky already growing dark from the smoke from
many fires, and as flaming ejecta crash around them, Alex,
Haupt, Featherstone and Bruce pull Bo from the toppled
Chrono-Cube.

>   BO
>   I'm OK.

They look down the slope–

The many small fires caused by the ejecta are swiftly com-
bining into one gigantic holocaust–and it's headed their way.

>   BRUCE
>   We've got to right the Cube fast!

All five men pitch in–but with all Haupt's equipment in it, it's
too heavy to lever upright–

They get the Cube partway up–then it topples back again
heavily–they leap out of the way.

>   ALEX
>   (to Haupt)
>   We've got to dump your equipment!

>   HAUPT
>   But–it's–

>   BO
>   It's us or it, Doc.

This sinks in–and Haupt starts tossing out his apparatus. Alex,
Bruce, Bo and Featherstone pitch in.

A Pteranodon, set aflame, crashes to Earth near them–they react, but go on with their desperate work.

Haupt pauses for a beat when he comes to his beloved spectro-telescope–then he hurls it, too, to the ground.

CUT TO:

EXT. FOREST SLOPE - DAY
Rivers drags Willow along. Small dinosaurs and mammals cross their path, running frightened in all directions.

The armored Ankylosaur from before runs crosswise toward them. Willow stumbles–Rivers loses hold of her.

He runs back for her–no time to pull her out of the way as the Ankylosaur thunders down upon them in its headlong fear–

At the last second, the Ankylosaur is struck by one of the fiery ejecta. It falls dead, head crashing to the ground within inches of Willow's leg.

Rivers pulls her up–they run onward. The deadly rain is di-minishing, but stray ejecta still fall. Trees are fewer further upslope, so only scattered fires before them.

Rivers looks back over his shoulder as they run–

Behind them, the forest fire is racing up the slope more swiftly than a man can run–igniting every tree, every shrub in its path from its sheer heat.

The T-Rex we saw before is briefly glimpsed through the fire, burning alive, writhing and then falling–

Several Triceratops flee like cattle before a wildfire–then are trapped between fires caused by two separate ejecta.

The Giganotosaurus, too, is retreating SNARLING before the flames.

Rivers pulls Willow along.

CUT TO:

EXT. CAMPSITE - DAY
With great effort, the men finally manage to right the Cube. Bruce winces as one side drops heavily into place.

BRUCE
Careful! If it's damaged, we're history.

HAUPT
You mean pre-history.

Several of the Stenonychosaurs from before come running terrified through camp–

BO
Watch out! Our little buddies are back!

Blinded by fear, one Steno runs into one of the Cube's plastiglass panels, knocking itself out–as the rest race on out of camp in search of non-existent safety.

BO
Now there's something you don't see every day.

He rolls the unconscious Steno onto the fallen tarpaulin, opens the Cube panel, and tosses both inside. Bruce reacts with horror, even amid the cataclysm:

BRUCE
What the hell are you doing?

                              BO
              Might as well save him for the zoo.

                            BRUCE
                       (no time to argue)
              Long as he won't come to before we're back.

Everyone scrambles into the Cube–they close the door. Haupt
and Featherstone give the unconscious Steno a wide berth.
Bruce fiddles the controls, but nothing lights up.

                            BRUCE
              It must've sustained some damage. I'll see if I
              can bypass it.

He furiously types commands. Abruptly, the lights begin to
function–the HUMMING rises, though more slowly than
usual.

                            BRUCE
                         (yelling)
              Ya-HOOOO!

Alex scans the distance–Bo puts a hand on his shoulder.

                              BO
              Alex, he was the best, but he's gone.

                            ALEX
                       (eyes widening)
              Like hell he is!

Bo turns to follow the line of Alex's gaze–

DOWNSLOPE
Seen from their POV–beyond the crevice, two Duckbill dinosaurs running toward them–they dart off to one side–

                              171

And, revealed behind them, Rivers and Willow are seen half-running, half-scrambling–framed by the light of the fire, and by smoke that rolls up from below–

THE CAMPSITE
The five in the Cube are elated to spy Rivers, but–

> BO
> He's still got to get across that crevice.

> ALEX
> (to Bruce)
> Give him a chance to reach us. Kill the power.

> BRUCE
> (surveying keyboard)
> The Cube's eating up energy like a sponge. If we kill the power, we won't be able to start up again.

Alex knows what this means–SHOUTS back toward Rivers:

> ALEX
> Come on, Rivers–you can make it!

DOWNSLOPE
Rivers and Willow are running toward the crevice–but now, out of the roiling smoke behind them, trampling on smaller beasts, emerges the ROARING Giganotosaurus.

CAMPSITE
The five time travelers gape, as the HUMMING slowly grows.

> BRUCE
> Holy shit!

Alex grabs up a .600 and aims it toward the Giganotosaurus as best he can, given his sprained arm. Bo deflects the gun barrel.

BO

No!

BRUCE

If you break our shielding, we're as good as dead.

ALEX

And if I don't fire, Rivers is!

Yet Alex hesitates, amid the rising HUM. Does he dare fire?

<u>AT THE CREVICE</u>

Rivers and Willow, running full out, nearly race right off the edge of the crevice before Rivers sees it–he barely stops her from falling in.

They look back at the Giganotosaurus bearing down on them– with the forest fire gaining on them all.

WILLOW

(looking off)

Hey, there's your big gun!

Rivers follows her gaze to the fallen .1000, lying a dozen or so yards away, near the lip of the crevice.

RIVERS

It won't help us get around this thing.

Just then, the Giganotosaurus blocks their view, as it stalks in between them and the rifle. It's after Rivers, even in this moment of fiery peril.

Rivers grabs a limb–like facing a tiger with a toothpick.

The Giganotosaurus rears, ready to swoop down at Rivers.

CAMPSITE - THE CHRONO-CUBE
The five in the Cube watch horrified amid the growing HUM–
the faint beginnings of the light-SHIMMER begin–more
slowly than usual, though they don't notice–

AT THE CREVICE
On an impulse, Willow suddenly races out from behind Rivers
and off down the hill–

The Giganotosaurus, drawn to motion, turns to pursue her–
leaving a yard or so distance between itself and the crevice–

Rivers does a running tumble over the Giganotosaurus' flail-
ing tail and rolls to where the .1000 lies.

Willow falls–the Giganoto looms above her, an instant from
swooping down with those mammoth, toothsome jaws–

Rivers comes up FIRING–BLAM!

A bloody hole appears over the Giganotosaurus' heart–mor-
tally wounded, it wavers to right and left–

For a moment, it looks as if it will fall on Willow–it sways,
back and forth, gushing blood–

–then it falls across the crevice so that its massive carcass becomes a natural bridge across the yawning abyss–its massive
head on the side near the Chrono-Cube.

CAMPSITE - THE CHRONO-CUBE
The five watchers react, amid the slow HUM and SHIMMER,
as the Giganotosaurus' fall shakes the Earth.

<u>AT THE CREVICE</u>
Rivers drops the .1000 and runs to Willow–helps her up.

> RIVERS
> That was dumb, running like that.

> WILLOW
> (saucy, even now)
> Gave you a chance to get to the gun, didn't it?

He scoops her up in his arms and looks downslope. The forest fire is almost upon them now–

> RIVERS
> You saying you did that on purpose?

> WILLOW
> (smiles)
> I'll never tell.

Rivers races off, carrying Willow, just ahead of the flames and the searing waves of heat.

The carcass of the Giganotosaurus spans the crevice, but precariously–it sags in the middle, and at any second it could topple into the abyss.

With Willow in his arms, Rivers runs up onto the Giganotosaurus' tail, flames licking his heels. Keeping his balance only with difficulty, he scrambles onto its carcass–

–and across the abyss, as the Giganotosaurus' body sags ever more greatly in the middle.

As they reach the far side of the crevice, atop the carnosaur's shoulder–

–suddenly the Giganotosaurus' huge head twists around–its great jaws open wide–it's still has a speck of life in it, and it means to kill Rivers–

Rivers dives off the beast with Willow–they reach solid ground, just barely, and roll clear of those CLAMPING jaws–

Next moment, the Giganotosaurus' writhing causes it to go hurtling down into the abyss–ROARING its dying defiance.

Rivers pulls Willow to her feet–

CAMPSITE
Its occupants are beckoning wildly to them, YELLING (un-heard behind plastiglass) to hurry.

Rivers starts to scoop her up again, but she pulls away and scrambles up on her own, ready to go.

WILLOW
I can walk from here.

Rivers grins–he and Willow race together toward the SHIM-MERING Chrono-Cube–

As Bruce operates the keyboard desperately–with difficulty, Bo forces the front panel open about a foot–the SHIMMER-ING nears de-materialization intensity–

Rivers and Willow leap in, pulled aboard by Alex and Bo–

At the last second, as Bo is pulling the door shut–Cyrano flies in, turning vertically to get through the space. He lands on Willow's forearm as the door closes–and SQUAWKS.

Alex looks O.S., and speaks in a low voice:

ALEX
Well, at least we don't have to worry about being killed by a forest fire.

The others follow his line of sight, and suddenly gape:

THEIR POV - THE FOREST FIRE
It's almost on top of them–a few dinosaurs can be glimpsed being engulfed by it, like bugs in a fireplace–flaming Ptero-saurs fall from the sky–

But, almost in the same instant, towering above the fire and dwarfing it, is a TSUNAMI–a huge tidal wave still hundreds of feet high even this far inland–it's drowning even the forest fire and heading straight for them!

CAMPSITE
The Chrono-Cube SHIMMERS in CENTER OF FRAME–as the ROARING forest fire, consuming the last vegetation atop the rise and feeding on itself, is about to engulf the Cube–

Then, the Tsunami thunders down over the fire–it's only a heartbeat from crashing into the Cube and smashing it to smithereens–

At that instant, once more the Chrono-Cube stays where it is–but the fiery, drowning world around it WINKS OUT OF EX-ISTENCE–to be instantly replaced by–

INT. CHRONO-LAB - DAY
The Cube (with occupants) again sits at the center of the spokes–Prochaska works his controls. Ming, Pandro and San-chez are there, anxious. The HUM and SHIMMER die.

The transparent door-panel opens–the occupants pour out. Bruce closes the door behind them.

Prochaska looks them over, surprised to see Rivers and Willow lean on each other as they exit—yet something is missing.

PROCHASKA
Where are Ms. Morgen—and Mr. Swayzey?

RIVERS
Afraid they won't be coming back.

Willow nestles against him.

ALEX
A long story, Professor.

MARV (O.S.)
Make it short.

All whirl, to see Marv and Lester, standing in the open doorway—grimly aiming handguns at them.

LESTER
Where's the boss?

As Marv covers them, Lester grabs Willow. With a SQUAWK, Cyrano hops back onto his perch, agitated. Rivers is clearly weighing attacking the pair's guns in spite of the odds.

MARV
Try it. I never thought you were such hot shit anyway.

RIVERS
(holding back)
Swayzey's dead. Kristen, or whatever her real name was, killed him. She was working for his enemies—you boys figure out which ones.

MARV

Don't bullshit us. You just left him behind, and we're
going back for him.

PROCHASKA

You're insane! You don't even know how to operate
the Transporter.

WILLOW

But I do.

Willow steps forward, her brazen manner returning. All react.

WILLOW (cont'd)

Hey, I spent four fade-outs watching Cohen press
buttons–most of it's automatic anyway.

LESTER

So Rivers is lying?

WILLOW

He left Des to die with the dinosaurs, but he was only
wounded. I can take you right to him.

MARV

If he's not all right, you're not makin' the return trip.

WILLOW

Imagine my surprise.

RIVERS
(starts forward)
Willow, no! You know what's–

Lester backhands Rivers in the jaw with his pistol. Rivers drops to one knee, bleeding from the mouth–a big part of him still wants to charge Lester and damn the consequences.

> WILLOW
> Forget him! Let's go.

> MARV
> (to Lester)
> You stay here and watch 'em.

Lester nods. Prochaska starts to object, but a look from Rivers makes him change what he says to Marv and Lester:

> PROCHASKA
> I'll do everything I can. After all, I don't want my Transporter damaged.

Marv moves with Willow toward the Cube. Both Bodyguards keep their guns trained especially on Rivers, Bo and Alex.

Willow opens the door, stepping back as she does so. To Marv:

> WILLOW
> After you.

Marv backs inside, pulling her with him, and closes the door, as Prochaska begins to operate his controls, lights flashing.

THE CHRONO-CUBE
As Marv keeps an eye on Rivers et al., Willow examines the Cube's keyboard: the keys marked "RETURN," "+," the numbered keys, and "HOURS." Marv is impatient:

MARV

Well? You know what to do, or do we drag that
Cohen guy in here?

WILLOW

Don't worry, I know what I'm doing.

She presses various keys—we don't see which ones. The Cube
begins to HUM, building. Marv is made very nervous by the
flashing lights and HUMMING.

Willow looks out at Rivers—

CHRONO-LAB
Prochaska operates his controls—Rivers, Alex, Bo, Bruce,
Haupt and Featherstone uneasy under Lester's watchful eye.

THE CHRONO-CUBE
The HUMMING rises, seconds away from the usual SHIM-
MERING and de-materialization. Willow is starting to get
uneasy herself.

Lester hears a HISS. He looks down and sees a tarpaulin on
the floor—something's moving beneath it. With the barrel of
his pistol, he lifts one end of the tarp.

The awakened Steno shoots out its skinny neck and jaws—its
fangs aren't especially long, but they sink into Marv's gunhand. He YELLS more in surprise than pain.

Like a shot, Willow flings open the door and leaps out.

CHRONO-LAB
The force of the hard-flung door makes it bounce closed
again—Marv is seen trying to disengage from the Steno, who's
probably as scared as he is—

181

Willow throws herself down onto the walkway as the HUM-MING crescendoes and the SHIMMERING BEGINS. She SHOUTS:

                    WILLOW
          Run!

Lester instinctively turns his gun toward her. Rivers leaps forward, grabbing his gunhand–and slugs him.

Lester topples SCREAMING off the walkway. It's a long way down.

As Alex and Bo shove Prochaska and the others out the door– the Cube SHIMMERS–Rivers rushes to Willow, scoops her up–

–and dives for the closing lab door just as the Chrono-Cube SHIMMERS at its brightest. Cyrano flies out with them.

The Cube SHIMMERS in CENTER OF FRAME a second longer–and then, in a maddening, lightning-fast SUCCES-SION OF IMAGES–

–the b.g. surrounding the Cube switches rapidly back and forth between Prochaska's lab, and the instant when the Cube left the Cretaceous: the moment when the forest fire reached the Cube, even as it was drowned by the tsunami!

Several times the background rapidly SHIFTS–from lab to Cretaceous cataclysm and back again–then the lab holds for a moment–

Next instant, the Cube EXPLODES IN SLOW MOTION– Cube debris and metal shards of spokes and computers tumble end over end in all directions–just as in Rivers' earlier dream! The lab is torn asunder–

INT. CORRIDOR - DAY

The heavy metal door marked "1" has been shoved shut–but it buckles under the force of the blast–buckles, and then blows.

The running Rivers and Willow are bringing up the rear as the others race for the main door at the far end of the corridor.

The effects of the explosion send them all reeling–head over heels, like weightless chaff. Some are thrown down or into other people–others hurled against the corridor walls. Cyrano is tossed end over end.

Rivers strives to shield Willow with his own body–he's slammed into a wall, and she slams into him–

And then it is over.

Rivers and Willow slide down the wall, coming to rest on the floor.

                         RIVERS
          You OK?

                         WILLOW
          Define "OK."

She smiles–Rivers realizes she's only shaken up. Cyrano hops onto her arm with a SQUAWK–he's ruffled, but OK.

Rivers looks around, sees the rest of the crew disentangling themselves. Ming, Pandro and Sanchez are unhurt.

Prochaska has a superficial cut on his forehead, but Bo examines it for a moment and makes an "A-OK" sign to Rivers.

A disheveled Bruce is leaning over Alex, who now has two sprained arms. Rivers and Willow move to them.

ALEX
(smiles at them)
Could be I'm getting too old for this business.
(beat)
I guess you didn't see any sign of Holtzinger
while you were out there?

Rivers hesitates–Willow looks to see what he'll say.

RIVERS
No. August Holtzinger died... a year before
I went looking for him.

He and Willow exchange a look. Rivers looks over at Haupt
and Featherstone–Haupt is helping Featherstone to his feet.

Haupt feels in his pockets, suddenly concerned. He looks
haplessly toward Rivers and Alex–

HAUPT
I lost my equipment–but I'd managed to transfer all
my data to a disk. Only, it must've fallen out back in–

A hopeless look comes over his face as he turns up nothing in
his pockets–was all this for nothing?

Featherstone's hand moves INTO FRAME, holding a disk.
Haupt reacts.

FEATHERSTONE
May I be the first to offer my congratulations... Einar.

Featherstone smiles wanly at Haupt. Haupt hugs him.

Rivers, relieved everyone's all right, moves off. Willow hurries to keep up with him. As they move to the crumpled doorway to the Chrono-Lab:

> RIVERS
> You really did pay attention at the Professor's
> press briefing.

> WILLOW
> So I set the controls for the same time we just left.

> RIVERS
> Did you know there was a passed-out Steno in there?

> WILLOW
> I'll never tell.

CHRONO-LAB - POV FROM INSIDE
Reaching the door, both gaze inside, framed by the shattered doorway. As they talk, CAMERA SLOWLY PULLS BACK–

–till the entire destroyed hollow sphere, with all its debris, fills the screen. It's as devastated as Lab #2 was.

> RIVERS
> If it hadn't revived, you'd have died saving our skin.

> WILLOW
> Maybe I just figured I'd never done much in my past
> that was worth writing home about.

He puts his finger gently to her lips.

> RIVERS
> The past is the past. Forget about it.

She takes his hand and kisses it, just as gently.

WILLOW

If you can forget the past, I guess I can. You've had
so many more to choose from.
(beat; looks into lab)
What'll happen to this place?

RIVERS

If Haupt's data spurs interest in time travel, I suspect
Prochaska's got enough spare parts to build a third
Chrono-Cube. It'll take a while, but we'll be back in
business. And when we are–

WILLOW

–you'll have all the time in the world.

RIVERS

Yeah.
(beat)
Yeah, maybe we will, at that...

Rivers puts his arm around Willow, as Cyrano flutters down to
land on her forearm–and the two of them walk away together,
lost to our sight beyond the shattered doorway.

We look down from the vacant doorway to examine the destroyed lab–till our view rests at last on a twisted shard of ma-
chinery lying atop the metal debris at the bottom.

The metal fragment abruptly HUMS slightly–and SHIM-
MERS–once briefly, then a bit longer–

–and then it WINKS OUT OF EXISTENCE.

FADE OUT.

THE END

ABOUT THE AUTHORS

Roy THOMAS has been a comic book writer (and often editor) since 1965, primarily for Marvel and DC. He was editor-in-chief of Marvel Comics from 1972 to 1974, and is particularly noted for his scripting of *Conan the Barbarian*, *The Avengers*, *X-Men*, *The Incredible Hulk*, *The Invaders*, *All-Star Squadron* and *Infinity, Inc*. In 2004-2005, for Marvel, Roy finished an adaptation, begun in 1974, of Bram Stoker's *Dracula*. In a major poll in the late 1990s, he was voted by pros and fans the fourth favorite editor and fifth favorite comic book writer of the 20th century. Between 1980-2000, Roy co-wrote and sold nine screenplays, of which two (*Conan the Destroyer* and *Fire and Ice*) were made into films. In addition to scripting comics, Roy continues to chronicle the medium's history in his acclaimed monthly magazine *Alter Ego*.